The Tablet

BOOK 4

Formerly titled *Journeys to Fayrah*

The Tablet

Bill Myers

TOMMY nelson™
FOR TWEENS AND TEENS

A Division of Thomas Nelson Publishers
Since 1798

www.thomasnelson.com

Book Four: The Tablet

Published in Nashville, Tennessee, by Tommy Nelson®, a Division of Thomas
Nelson, Inc. Visit us on the Web at www.tommynelson.com.

Scripture quotations are from the *International Children's Bible*®, *New Century
Version*®, copyright © 1986, 1988, 1999 by Tommy Nelson®, a Division of
Thomas Nelson, Inc.

Tommy Nelson® books may be purchased in bulk for educational, business,
fund-raising, or sales promotional use. For information, please e-mail us at
SpecialMarkets@ThomasNelson.com.

This is a work of fiction. Names, characters, places, and incidents either are the
product of the author's imagination or are used fictitiously.

Book design: Mark & Jennifer Ross / MJ Ross Design

ISBN 1-4003-0747-3

Printed in the United States of America
05 06 07 08 09 WRZ 9 8 7 6 5 4 3 2 1

For Dale Evrist . . .
a man of truth, commitment,
and integrity

Book 4
The Tablet
CONTENTS

Book 4
The Tablet

Chapter One

The Signal

"DENNNYYYYYY . . ."

Denise Wolff twisted and turned in the chair beside her mom's hospital bed. For the third time that night she dreamed of how her mother had fallen off the ladder. For the third time that night she saw her tumbling like a Barbie doll from their second-story window. And for the third time she heard the crack of shrubs and the sickening thud of her mother hitting the ground.

"Mom . . . *Mom!*"

No answer.

Denise raced toward the bushes, a coldness already knotting in her stomach. "*MOTHER!*"

She found her sprawled out on the ground, trying to catch her breath. "I'm all right, Denny," she gasped. "I'm all right, it's okay."

But it wasn't okay. Denise could see that in a second. It wasn't okay the way her mom kept trying to breathe but couldn't. And it wasn't okay the way one of her legs was twisted and pointed in the wrong direction.

Mom had been trying to change the storm windows, as she did every spring. Of course, if there was a husband around the house, she wouldn't have had to. Then again, if there was a husband around, they'd probably have enough money to buy windows that didn't need changing.

But Mom had no husband—at least not anymore. And Denise had no father—at least not one she could remember. He'd left when she was four.

Now it was just the two of them—mother and daughter. Of course, they had their fights—like over the torn and baggy clothes Denise always wore. But the two loved each other fiercely. And when the chips were down, they always knew the other would be there.

And that afternoon "being there" meant Denise calling 911, riding with Mom in the ambulance, pacing in the waiting room, and listening to the doctors say she had some bruised ribs and a shattered leg.

Everybody told Denise to go home and get some rest. "Your mother will be fine," they said. "She's under mild sedation—she'll barely know you're here."

But Denise wouldn't listen and she wouldn't leave. She'd already lost one parent; she wasn't about to lose another. Instead, she borrowed a blanket and pillow from an adjacent room and tried to get comfortable in the steel and vinyl chair next to Mom's bed.

Here she waited. And here her world-famous anger started to burn. . . .

Why had Mom fallen?

Why did things always go wrong?

Why was life always so hard?

Of course, Denise knew Imager loved her. After all, she'd been to the Center. She'd even been re-Breathed. But sometimes that love seemed so far away. Sometimes it seemed as if Imager had forgotten, or that he didn't know, or, worse yet, that he simply didn't care.

"It would be a whole lot different if I were in charge," she mumbled as she drifted in and out of a fitful sleep. "A *whole* lot different."

The thought churned in her mind—of being in charge, of being the boss.

The Signal

Unfortunately, she had no idea that the thought would trigger a little alarm—a little alarm for a creature who had sworn revenge upon her—a creature on the molten hot surface of Ecknolb. . . .

TeeBolt! Come quickly!" cried the Merchant of Emotions. "It's happening, it's happening!"

The Merchant turned from his monitors and chuckled as he watched the huge, hairy TeeBolt gallop toward him. The animal's eight furry legs raced across the steaming rocks as fast as they could. He would have barked and yelped in pain, but he had nothing to bark and yelp with. In an outburst of anger the Merchant had destroyed TeeBolt's vocal chords many epochs ago.

"Look, my pet, it's the Denise—the creature who destroyed our Illusionist!" The Merchant of Emotions threw his claws up in joy. He fluttered his wings in delight. The Illusionist had been his sister—until Denise accidentally destroyed her in the Sea of Justice. Ever since then, the Merchant had vowed vengeance. Not only upon Denise, but upon all of her kind, upon all Upside Downers. The only problem was, he had been confined to the desolate planet of Ecknolb, forbidden ever to enter the Upside-Down Kingdom—at least on his own. At least without an invitation.

But all that was changing. For months he'd been monitoring Denise's thoughts, waiting for the opportunity. Now it was here . . . the beginning of distrust, the seed of rebellion. "The Denise is doubting!" the Merchant chortled with excitement. "What a fool. The Denise thinks it knows more than Imager!"

Of course, TeeBolt had no idea what his master was saying or why he was so excited. But it made little difference. The Merchant simply glanced down to the Emotion Generator strapped to his chest, scanned the dozens of silver switches, and flipped the one labeled "excitement." A misty cloud shot from the contraption's nozzle. It struck TeeBolt dead center and filled him with so much *excitement* that he couldn't contain himself. He was so thrilled that he began leaping on the Merchant and panting. The only trouble was that when he panted he drooled.

"Get down, you nincompoop! Stop that slobbering!"

Immediately TeeBolt hopped down and closed his mouth. For if he didn't hop down and close his mouth, he might not have any legs to hop down on or a mouth to close.

"Now if I can just get the Denise to dream about the Tablet—if I can just convince the Denise to begin writing on it." The Merchant spun back to the monitor before him and adjusted several dials. "Then the Denise will invite us into her world. Then I will get my claws on the Tablet. And then"—he began to grin—"then we will finally be able to destroy her wretched little world."

The Merchant broke into laughter. The joy of destroying Imager's precious Upside-Down Kingdom caused every crystal scale on his body to quiver with delight. TeeBolt was still too overwhelmed with *excitement* to understand the humor . . . until the Merchant reached down and snapped on the *laughter* switch.

Another cloud of mist shot out and struck TeeBolt. The animal began to laugh uncontrollably. He couldn't help himself. That was the power the Merchant of Emotions had over TeeBolt—over all creatures who gave him control. And it was this power that had been banned from the Upside-Down Kingdom.

But even from great distances he could sometimes direct dreams. Not a lot, mind you. But if the dreamer was angry enough, if there was enough rebellion in their hearts, then there might be room for the Merchant to nudge some of their dreams in his direction. He might even be able to influence a waking thought or two.

The Signal

That's exactly what he hoped to accomplish with the Denise. That's exactly how he hoped to enter and destroy her world.

▣

Back in Grandpa O'Brien's Secondhand Shop, Joshua and Nathan were arguing again. Like Denise, they'd both visited Fayrah. They'd both been re-Breathed. And they'd both started to grow in Imager's ways. But when it came to good old-fashioned brotherly bickering . . . well, these guys were pros.

"You're the oldest," Nathan whined.

"So?"

"So, till Grandpa gets back from deliveries, let *me* visit Denny and *you* stay to look after the shop."

"No way," Josh argued as he stooped to adjust his hair in the reflection of a used toaster. "All you and Denny ever do is fight. She needs me at the hospital—somebody more mature and sensitive to look after her."

"Oh, please," Nathan groaned. He turned and limped toward the counter. His hip, the one that had bothered him since birth, was acting up again. But he wouldn't let his brother see the pain. No way. Not when he had an argument to win.

They'd been going around like this ever since Denise had phoned from the hospital, and they were no closer to an agreement than when they started. As far as Nathan knew, the only person more stubborn than himself was his brother. And according to Joshua, the only person more stubborn than himself was Nathan. So around and around they went . . . and around some more.

Fortunately, the standoff was about to end. Because suddenly they heard a very familiar voice.

**Now come on, little buddies,
don't get in a dither.
Put aside all yer fighting,
and let us draw hither.**

The brothers exchanged looks. Only one person in the universe had such awful poetry.

"Aristophenix!" they shouted.

Next came the familiar . . .

BEEP!........BOP!........BLEEP!.......BURP!....

. . . of three very good friends cross-dimensionalizing into their world.

And finally . . .

"Get us down—get us down from here!"

The brothers looked up to see Aristophenix, a roly-poly creature with checkered vest and walking stick, and Listro Q, a tall purple dude complete with a Mohawk and a tuxedo, spinning high above their heads. Apparently Listro Q's aim with the Cross-Dimensionalizer hadn't improved much. He and Aristophenix were caught on the ceiling fan, spinning round and round.

"Won't you—*whoa*—ever get—*whoo*—the hang of that thing?" Aristophenix cried.

"Cool, is it," Listro Q shouted. "Any day now, sure of it am I."

The third member of the party wasn't caught on the fan. He was darting about their heads chattering a mile a minute. Or was he laughing? It was hard to tell with Samson. The part ladybug, part dragonfly talked so fast it was hard to tell anything he said.

Nathan raced to the switch on the wall and turned off the fan.

Aristophenix didn't wait for it to stop.

The Signal

Thank ya, dear Nathan,
there ain't a second to waste.
The Weaver, he's a-callin',
so we'd better make haste.

Joshua and Nathan traded glances. The Weaver—the kind old gentleman assigned by Imager to weave their life's tapestries—was calling *them* to Fayrah!

"But what about Denise?" Nathan asked. "Doesn't he want her to come, too?"

Denny's the reason
we're under such stress.
She's dreamin' up somethin'
that's causin' a mess.

Again Joshua and Nathan exchanged looks.

"We can't leave just yet," Joshua said. "Not till Grandpa gets back from his deliveries."

"Worry don't about the store," Listro Q answered. "This part of world, freeze time will we."

From past adventures, Joshua could pretty much piece together his words. "You mean you're going to freeze time again and make it stand still?" he asked.

"But here only at the store. Rest of world will it be normal time."

Samson gave a quick chatter.

Aristophenix nodded. "Good thinkin', Sammy."

"What's he saying?" Nathan asked.

Listro Q translated. "Mr. Hornsberry, here is he?"

"My stuffed bulldog?" Nathan asked. "No, he's at home."

"Then swing by your home, better do we."

7

"Why?"

Aristophenix explained,

> **This adventure's gonna be tricky,**
> **but his help we can't skip.**
> **We'll just have to endure**
> **his snooty and snobby lip.**

Nathan had to admit, his stuffed bulldog *was* snooty. And he was a snob. But from all the excitement, it sounded like they were going to need all the man and dog power they could get.

"Canteen of Imager's water," Listro Q asked, "still have you?"

"Not anymore," Josh replied. "We used it all up in that ocean of mirrors."

"Then loan you my own," Listro Q said as he removed a large water skin from around his neck.

Joshua took it and quickly slipped it around his shoulders.

"Ready to go are we, if are you." Listro Q said as he held the Cross-Dimensionalizer in his hand.

The brothers nodded. Without a word Listro Q punched in the four coordinates . . .

BEEP!........B^{o}P!........BLEEP!.......BURP!....

. . . and they were off.

Chapter Two

Dream On

Denise woke with a start. For a minute she didn't know where she was—until she felt the jab of a steel armrest in her ribs, the sticky vinyl against her arms, and the cramp in her neck.

Ah, yes, the hospital chair.

She looked over at her sleeping mom. The sedative was still working. In fact, in the dim morning light her mother looked peaceful, almost happy. It was a look Denise hadn't seen for years. Not from Mom. And for some reason it made her throat ache with sadness.

"Life is hard, then you die." That's what Mom always said. Of course, it was supposed to be funny, but Denise knew better. All she had to do was look where they were this minute to see that it was no joke. Life *was* hard. *Too* hard.

Once again she felt the frustration stirring inside. Frustration at what had happened. Frustration at their life in general. If Imager was supposed to be so loving, then why were things always so hard? Why was there always so much pain? Why was there any suffering at all?

Stewing in her anger, she recalled the dream. Not the dream about the ladder, but the other one. She had no idea where it came from. It seemed so strange and yet so real.

In it she was upstairs all alone in her uncle's attic. A large black trunk sat in front of her. Slowly, she knelt down to it. This is where she'd found the Bloodstone. This is where she and Nathan had found Bud's cassette tape. And this is where the two of them had discovered the flat, thin stone at the very bottom.

Carefully, she had lifted the trunk's heavy lid. It groaned in protest. On the top were clothes. Lots and lots of clothes. She began digging through them until she reached the bottom, until she finally felt it—the cold, smooth stone. She hauled it to the surface and set it on the pile of clothes. It was exactly as she remembered—a big, flat rock—super thin and super smooth.

What she did not remember were the faint green lines running across the stone—like notebook paper—like it was some sort of writing tablet.

Suddenly, a felt marker appeared in her hand. And then . . . . Well, then the dream was over—just like that. There was nothing more. It had ended and she woke up. And yet it remained in her mind, just as clear as ever.

"Weird," Denise sighed. She glanced over at her mom, then turned in her chair to go back to sleep.

But sleep wouldn't come. Not anymore. There was something about the dream, something so real about that stone. She lay in the chair wide awake, staring into the dark . . . wondering.

She didn't know how long she lay there—twenty minutes, an hour. But finally, she'd had enough. Throwing off the blanket, she looked at her watch.

6:50.

She hated to cross town and wake up her aunt this early. She knew the lady would think she was strange. Then again, everyone thought she was strange, so what was one more person added to the list?

Denise turned back to Mom. She was still sleeping. "I'll be back in a few minutes," she whispered. "I just gotta check something."

With that, Denise uncurled herself from the chair, grabbed her jacket, and headed for the door.

◨

Dream On

By now Joshua and Nathan were pretty used to traveling across dimensions. They were used to the blinding light and the sensation of falling. They were even used to seeing themselves as Imager saw them—Joshua as some sort of water bearer in a burlap robe and Nathan as a knight in a glowing suit of armor just a few sizes too big, carrying a heavy shield.

Master Nathan, Master Nathan . . .

He turned to see Mr. Hornsberry, his stuffed bulldog, traveling beside him. Moments earlier they had dropped by Nathan's bedroom to pick him up. Back there he was just as dead and lifeless as any other stuffed dog. But here he was alive and back to his usual snooty self.

How you doing, Mr. Hornsberry? Nathan thought (since speaking wasn't necessary when Cross-Dimensionalizing).

As well as might be expected, having been confined to your closet these many months.

Sorry about—

I trust you're aware of the distinct aroma those gym socks in the corner have been emitting.

Before Nathan could answer, Aristophenix interrupted,

**Good to see ya, ol' boy,
but we're a comin' to the Center.
Best be thinkin' them good thoughts,
so more gently you'll enter.**

Nathan glanced down and saw they were approaching the brightly lit city. From past experiences, he knew what to do. Like the others, he closed his eyes and began thinking of Imager's greatness. Ever so faintly he could hear Aristophenix starting to sing. Someone else in the group was humming. Others quietly whispered. But no matter what they did, their purpose was the same —to dwell on Imager's greatness, to join with the rest of the universe in their love and adoration of him.

Soon they passed through a thin layer of fog and moments later they landed in the Center.

Nathan looked about in awe. Although he'd been to the Center before, his reaction was always the same: wonder and astonishment. He was amazed at the beautiful lights, the incredible colors. But they were more than just lights and colors . . . they were living creatures. Living creatures that reflected Imager's greater light, his greater color. A greater light and color that blazed brilliantly just over the ridge.

Then there was the music. It came from everywhere—the trees, the grass, even their own bodies. Everything vibrated with marvelous chords and intricate melodies—all directed toward Imager.

But this time something was different. "Nathan!" Josh cried. "Look at us! We're not shadows anymore. We're real!"

Nathan looked at Josh, then down at himself. It was true. In their past visits to the Center they had only been misty shadows. It's not that they weren't real, it's just that everything around them had been so much *more* real. But now, all of that had changed.

"You're right," Nathan cried, tapping his armor. "You can't see through me! I'm totally here! We're both totally here!"

Samson buzzed their heads and chattered an explanation. Aristophenix translated,

> It's 'cause you're re-Breathed,
> now you've got Imager's Presence.
> You're no longer just shadows,
> since you're Filled with his Essence.

Dream On

"'Cause his Breath is inside us?" Josh asked. "That's what makes us real?"

Listro Q nodded. "Ever since Whirlwind filled you, as real now you are as . . ." He turned toward the light glowing behind the ridge. "As Imager."

Nathan looked back toward the ridge and the blazing light behind it—a light so brilliant that it made all the others dim by comparison. But he knew it was more than just light. It had a quality . . . a *splendor*. A splendor so intense that it nearly destroyed Denise on an earlier trip.

"Aristophenix?" Joshua called. "Could we see him now? Now that we're solid and real and everything . . . would it be safe to see Imager?"

Nathan turned to him. "Are you crazy? You know what happened when Denny tried to see him!"

"But it's different now," Joshua insisted. "We're re-Breathed." He turned to Listro Q and Aristophenix. "Right?"

The Fayrahnians exchanged looks. It was obvious they were in a hurry, but it was also obvious they didn't want to deprive either of the brothers from experiencing more of Imager.

Samson chattered something, and with a heavy sigh Aristophenix agreed.

> **Well, if that's what you want,**
> **I ain't gonna spoil it.**
> **But we gotta hurry and save**
> **yer world from, uh . . . the toilet!**

The group groaned as they started toward the ridge.

◙

Denise heaved open the lid to the trunk. It gave a heavy

groan—just like her dream. She peered inside and began digging through the clothes—just like the dream.

Her aunt, a frail lady, stood at the top of the attic stairs clutching her robe against the morning chill. She watched silently as Denise plowed through the old clothes and oddities.

"What's this?" Denise asked as she pulled out the camera she and Nathan had seen on their last visit to the trunk. As best she could tell it had no lens and it was impossible to tell the front from the back.

"You know your uncle," the woman sighed. "Just something he brought back from one of his trips. We'll have to ask him when he returns."

Denise looked at her. The woman smiled weakly. Her husband had been gone over two years. At first he'd returned from his documentary filmmaking ventures with strange and weird tales about strange and weird places. Then one day he disappeared and never returned at all. Everyone knew he wasn't coming back—everyone but his wife. Well, maybe she knew, too. Maybe she just wanted to keep hoping.

At last Denise reached the bottom of the trunk. There was a rusty jackknife and a beat-up pair of sunglasses. But it was the large, smooth stone that had her attention. It was about the size of a yellow legal pad and almost as thick.

Carefully she pulled it out. It was exactly as she remembered from the last time she was there, and almost the same as her dream.

"Almost" because there were no faint green lines on this rock. Nor was there any marker pen. She scowled slightly.

"What's wrong, honey?" her aunt asked.

"Something's not right."

Without a word she plowed through the trunk again.

But she found nothing new.

Dream On

She plopped down on the floor, cross-legged. Pulling the tablet onto her lap, she began drumming her fingers on it, trying to think. The surface was smooth and hard, but not so hard that she couldn't make faint marks with her fingernails.

Her aunt turned and started down the steps. "Why don't I go and fix us some nice hot chocolate," she said.

Denise thanked her and continued to ponder. She knew it had only been a dream. But everything seemed so real, so true. So why weren't the lines there? And the marker? As she sat thinking, she absentmindedly began scratching her name onto the soft stone with her fingernail.

First a D . . . then an E . . . followed by an N . . .

It was no big deal, just faint markings she could easily wipe away. But when she scratched in the final letter . . . it happened!

There was somebody else in the room.

She spun around, then sucked in her breath—not because she was frightened; the person in front of her wasn't frightening at all. It was not some strange creature from some strange dimension. In fact, she knew this person very well. Very well indeed. Because standing directly in front of Denise Wolff stood . . . Denise Wolff!

Somehow, by writing her name on the tablet, Denise had created another Denise . . . exactly like herself!

Chapter Three

A Little Stopover

Even with his clumsy suit of armor and heavy shield, Nathan was only a few steps behind Josh as they raced for the top of the hill. He wasn't crazy about the idea of seeing Imager, but he was even less crazy about being left behind.

Suddenly there was a blinding flash of light just on the other side.

"What's that?" Josh cried.

Aristophenix was pulling up the rear by a dozen yards. His pudgy little body couldn't keep pace with the others, but between wheezes he managed to gasp,

> **Must be graduation (pant, puff)**
> **for Upside Downers, take a peek.**
> **Go see what's in store (wheeze, gasp)**
> **when your lives are complete.**

Joshua and Nathan reached the top of the ridge just in time to be hit by another flash of light. It was so bright, so intense, that it knocked both of them to the ground. Being the scientific type, Josh found it difficult to believe that light could actually knock a person down. But when he found himself lying face first in the dirt it was a lot easier to accept. This light had *presence*—so pure, so intense, that it carried with it incredible power.

Since he was already on the ground, and since he was scared to death, he figured it wouldn't hurt to lie there just a bit longer. No real reason except that he enjoyed living and he wasn't sure that would continue if he got up. So there he stayed,

A Little Stopover

cowering on the ground, covering his head right alongside his brother.

But not forever. Call it scientific curiosity or just plain stupidity, he wasn't sure. It didn't matter. The point was Josh *had* to see. He *had* to know what was going on. So, with eyes still clinched and head still covered, he leaned to Nathan and whispered, "We should really take a look."

"Are you nuts?" Nathan's voice echoed from under his shield.

"We just can't stay on our faces."

"Oh, I bet we can," Nathan said. "I got a few more things I want to do before I croak."

"Imager's not going to kill us."

"How do you know?"

"Listro Q says he's too cool, too loving. Come on, don't you want to take a little peek?"

"I'll take their word for it. Just lie here and keep quiet."

With eyes still shut, Joshua turned his head and called, "Aristophenix?"

"Josh, will you keep—"

"Aristophenix . . . Listro Q?"

There was no answer. Only another flash. A flash so bright that even with his eyes closed Josh could feel its power wash over him.

That was it. He could stand no more. Live or die (although living still had a lot more appeal) Josh had to see. Still clinching his eyes shut, he slowly turned toward the light.

So far so good. No heart attack. No vaporization. These were all encouraging signs.

Finally, he pried open one eye. Off to his left, Aristophenix, Listro Q, Samson, even Mr. Hornsberry, were all on their knees, faces bowed to the ground in the direction of the light. Carefully, he opened his other eye and slowly shifted his gaze toward the light. It grew brighter and brighter but he kept forcing himself. He knew the dangers of looking into the sun, but somehow this was different. The back of his eyes started to ache, but he pressed on. He had to. He shielded his eyes as he continued to look until finally, at last, Joshua O'Brien was gazing directly into the light.

And in it he saw . . .

Nothing.

Well, at first nothing. It was too bright to see anything. But as he squinted, he slowly made out a large, broad plain that stretched below them. It was so clear and smooth that it looked like water. But it couldn't be water. There were too many creatures standing on it. Millions of glowing creatures.

And they were singing. They were all singing to an even brighter Figure standing in the center of the plain—a Figure carved out of the most intense, blazing light imaginable. Light brighter than the sun. Brighter than a thousand suns.

Josh squinted harder. You didn't have to be a genius to figure out who the Figure was. At first it stood directly in the middle of the plain. Then, suddenly, it was standing much closer. Then far off in the distance. Then somewhere to Josh's left. Then to his right. It was pretty confusing. As if it were everywhere at the same time.

Then there was its face.

Actually, it was too bright to see the face, but there was no missing the profile—a profile that kept changing. One minute it was a giant bird, like an eagle; the next, some sort of bull; then an innocent lamb, followed by a lion. Back and forth it changed, again and again and again.

It was too much to comprehend. Josh's head began spinning.

A Little Stopover

Everything was too strange, too weird. He grew dizzy, his brain overloading. Then suddenly he heard a voice. It shook the ground like thunder, so loud that it made his ears ring. Yet it was softer than a whisper.

"HELLO, JOSHUA."

Josh spun around and gasped. The Figure was kneeling directly beside him! His head reeled. Instinctively, he bowed to the ground. Still, he had to see. He had to look into the face. Slowly, and with great terror, he forced himself to raise his head. When their gaze finally met, he saw eyes as powerful as the voice . . . *and* as tender. They blazed with fire—a fire that burned deep into Joshua's mind.

He could not look away, even if he wanted.

The eyes held him. They searched his thoughts—seeing inside to his deepest, darkest secrets. Things no one knew. Things he did in secret, said in secret, thought in secret. Things that embarrassed him. Suddenly they were all exposed by the light. Every thought and action of Joshua O'Brien was in plain view of those eyes.

But he felt no fear. Because, as penetrating as those eyes were, as much as they saw his darkest secrets, they didn't condemn those secrets. If anything, they seemed to love and understand Josh more *because* of those secrets.

It took Joshua forever to find his voice. When he did it came out as a little squeak. "Who . . ." But that was as far as he got. He was too overcome to talk.

The Figure seemed to understand. He motioned toward the plain below them, toward all the different appearances of himself.

"I AM HE."

Josh wasn't sure if he was going to lose his mind or just die. But for some reason he did neither. It had something to do with the way those marvelous eyes held him.

He tried to ask another question. "How . . ." But he shook his head. He had no business asking anything. He had no business saying anything. At that moment he had no business *being* anything.

The eyes looked on kindly. The voice roared and whispered:

"ASK YOUR QUESTION, JOSHUA O'BRIEN."

Josh swallowed hard and tried again. "How . . . how can you be here . . . and down there at the same time? You're everywhere at once."

"YES, I AM."

"But . . . one minute you're a bird, then an animal, then—"

**"YOUR MIND CANNOT GRASP MY FULLNESS,
SO IT SEES ME IN SYMBOLS."**

"But—"

"BEHOLD . . ."

The Figure pointed to a withered old woman on the plain below them. Unlike the others, she was shriveled and crippled. And, unlike the others, she was *not* glowing. He continued speaking, his voice lowered in quiet reverence:

**"SHE'S AN UPSIDE DOWNER . . .
LIKE YOU."**

"You mean she's cross-dimensionalized just like—"

"NO. SHE HAS GRADUATED."

"Graduated?"

"BEHOLD."

Joshua looked back at the plain. The glowing Figure of Light was now standing beside the woman. Josh looked back at his side. The Figure of Light was also there. "Okay," he mumbled, trying to get a grip. "I can handle this. I hope . . ."

He turned back to the plain and watched as the old woman crumpled at the Figure's feet and began sobbing. But she wasn't the only one crying. So was the Figure.

A Little Stopover

A hush fell over the plain. All singing came to a stop. The millions of creatures watched in speechless anticipation as the Figure slowly stooped down to join the old woman. At last he spoke:

"I HAVE BEEN WAITING A LONG TIME FOR YOU."

The woman looked up. Tears streamed down her face. Tears streamed down both of their faces. Slowly, the Figure reached out his hands and helped her as they rose to their feet. Smiling, he wiped the tears from her cheeks. She looked up into his eyes, her face glowing in love and adoration. Then gently, tenderly, he pulled her into a deep embrace.

And with that embrace . . . came another flash of light!

Josh ducked his head as the wave of power roared over him. When it was finally safe, he looked back up and saw the woman was still in the Figure's arms. But she was different now . . . much different. Now, she glowed. Now, she shared a part of the Figure's brilliance—a part of his power. No longer was she bent and crippled. Now she was beautiful. Radiant. Now she was young, vibrant, and glowing with the Figure's own glory.

The two separated but continued gazing into each other's eyes like lovers who'd been apart for years. Finally the Figure took her hand into his. He said only four words.

"COME, SIT WITH ME."

The entire plain broke into applause . . . then shouts and cheers as the couple turned and headed through the throng.

Josh looked on, his own eyes burning with tears. The back of his throat hurt with emotion. He turned to the Figure of Light who was now beside him. He tried to speak, his voice hoarse and raspy. "Do you . . . do that . . . with everyone?"

There was no missing the moisture in the Figure's eyes as he smiled.

"I DO THAT WITH MY FRIENDS."

Back in the attic Denise stared at the newly created Denise. But, never known for her shyness, the first Denise immediately demanded, "Who are you?"

"I'm you," the new Denise answered.

"You mean you're a picture of me—like a holograph."

"No, I'm you."

"But . . . how?"

"How should I know? You're the one who wrote me."

"Wrote . . . ?"

"Didn't you just write my name on the Tablet?"

Denise looked at the flat stone on her lap. "Well, no—how could I? I don't have anything to write—"

"With your fingernail," the new Denise sighed. "You just scratched my name on the Tablet with your fingernail."

"So?"

"So here I am."

"You mean . . . whatever I write on this thing—"

"—happens. Yeah."

"Let me get this straight. You're saying that whatever I write on this *Tablet* becomes real?"

The new Denise shook her head and muttered, "I didn't know I could be so ignorant. Yes! Yes! Whatever you write on that Tablet becomes—"

But she never finished . . . for immediately Denise reached over and rubbed off the name and immediately the second Denise disappeared.

She took a deep breath and blew it out. A little unsteady, she rose to her feet. Was this really happening? Could this thing . . .

A Little Stopover

this *Tablet* . . . really create anything she wrote? Balancing the stone on one hand, she started to scratch in her name again until she noticed her fingernail was wearing thin. She changed her mind. Instead, she wrote: FELT PEN.

Instantly there was a black marker in her hand . . . just like the dream.

Denise blinked in surprise. She stared at the marker. Was this really true? And if it *was*, what did it mean? What were the limits? *Were* there limits? Possibilities filled her mind. She frowned and gripped the marker tighter. After a moment's thought, she started to scrawl out the letters *C-A-R* but stopped. She paused, and quickly wrote *L-I-M-O-U-S-I-N-E*, instead.

When she had finished, she looked down at the word, took another deep breath, and quickly walked to the window for a look. Sure enough—outside, parked in front of the house, was a black, shiny limo.

Denise leaned against the wall for support. This was too incredible. With the Tablet it looked like she could make anything she wanted—mansions, yachts, castles. But material things had never interested her much (well, except for a limo or two). One look at her wardrobe said that.

Then why, she wondered, was she the one given the . . . wait a minute. Of course. That was it, that's why she'd had the dream. That's why she'd been led to the Tablet. It wasn't so she could make her own selfish desires come true. No, of course not. It was so she could help make things better in the world!

The thought gave her a little shudder. She breathed harder, faster. What a privilege. She, Denise Wolff, had been chosen to change the world! Think of it. She would have the opportunity to make things better, to do away with suffering, to stop violence, to end starvation, disease, and poverty. She could actually help make things . . . *perfect*! This was no "genie in a lamp" time—no "make three wishes and get whatever you want." Forget the riches, forget the fame. Denise was chosen because she would do something greater. She would fix the world!

She felt the weight of the Tablet in her hands—its power, its possibilities. But where to begin? The world was in such a mess; where should she start?

How about something small? she thought. *Yeah, that's it. For starters, I should begin with something*—She had it! If she wanted to end all pain and suffering, how about starting off with her mother? Mom, who was filled with so much pain at the hospital.

She raised the Tablet and wrote the words: *NO PAIN*.

She finished and waited in anticipation. But nothing happened. Everything was exactly the same. She glanced back out the window. The limo was still there. Nothing else had changed. Or had it? There was only one way to find out.

She turned and headed for the stairs.

▣

Joshua didn't know how long their conversation lasted. It could have been hours, it could have been seconds. But by the way Nathan, Aristophenix, and the gang were still on their knees, he voted for seconds.

The blazing Figure of Light continued speaking, his voice powerfully tender:

**"MY BELOVED UPSIDE-DOWN KINGDOM
IS IN DANGER."**

"Yes," Josh answered, "I know, but how—"

"DEAR DENISE."

Josh thought he heard a heavy sigh.

A Little Stopover

**"SHE NO LONGER TRUSTS ME.
SHE IS CREATING A DIFFERENT WORLD.
A WORLD SHE THINKS IS BETTER THAN MINE.
A WORLD WHERE SHE WILL INVITE
THE MERCHANT OF EMOTIONS."**

"Merchant of Emotions?"

**"HE WHO CONTROLS THROUGH EMOTIONS.
THAT IS WHY YOU AND YOUR BROTHER MUST
HELP."**

Josh's mouth dropped open. "What . . . what can we do?"

The Figure smiled.

**"YOU WILL DEFEAT HIM.
AS MY WATER BEARER, YOU HAVE MY WORD.
AS MY ARMOR BEARER, NATHAN HAS MY FAITH.
TOGETHER YOU TWO WILL HELP
MY DENISE UNDERSTAND."**

"Yes, but why don't—"

"WHY DON'T I STOP HER?"

Joshua nodded.

"MY DENISE NO LONGER LISTENS TO ME."

"You could make her."

The briefest look of pain flickered across those magnificent eyes.

**"SHE MUST TRUST ME BECAUSE SHE WANTS TO,
NOT BECAUSE I MAKE HER."**

Then, reaching out a hand, the Figure gently helped Joshua to his feet.

Of course, Josh wanted to say more . . .

. . . like, the only thing he and his brother had ever succeeded at doing together was fighting, so how could they save the world?

. . . like, shouldn't Imager chose someone else?

. . . like, did he really need *their* help?

But Josh didn't say a word. He knew Imager already knew. Now he felt his tender, powerful hand resting upon his shoulder.

"YOU ARE MY FEET, JOSHUA O'BRIEN.
YOU ARE MY HANDS.
YOU ARE MY VOICE."

Never in his life had Joshua felt so proud . . . or so helpless.

As if sensing his fear, the Figure drew him into an gentle embrace. There was no flash of light. No transfer of energy. No "graduation." Only the warmth and love of Imager holding his Beloved. It was fantastic. Joshua wanted to stay in that embrace forever. But he knew he couldn't, at least not now.

Finally they separated. Josh brushed the tears from his eyes and looked up just in time to catch the Figure doing the same.

"Will I . . . ever see you again?" Josh croaked.

The Figure broke into a gentle grin.

"YES, MY DEAR FRIEND, YOU WILL SEE ME.
YOU WILL SEE ME WHEREVER YOU LOOK."

With that Joshua suddenly found himself standing in Fayrah. No cross-dimensionalizing, no traveling—one minute he was standing before Imager; the next, he and the entire group stood in one of Fayrah's Great Halls of Tapestry.

Chapter Four

Changes

The Halls of Tapestry were as dazzling as ever. In every room hung thousands of tapestries—beautiful, shimmering tapestries woven from glowing threads of light. Each was a masterpiece. Each represented a life Imager had created. Every living creature imagined had his or her own tapestry hanging in one of these magnificent halls.

Nathan was the first to spot the Weaver. The old man was pacing back and forth between tapestries at the far end of the room. Even from that distance Nathan could tell he was concerned.

As the group approached, the Weaver glanced up. "You're late" was all he said before he returned to his pacing.

Aristophenix tried to explain,

**They wanted to see Imager,
a request we could not shrug.
And by the glow on Josh's face,
it was somethin' he dug.**

The Weaver shuddered. Apparently even he could not get used to the awful poetry.

"What's the problem?" Nathan asked as he approached, clinking and clanking in his armor. "And why are we still wearing these outfits? We usually lose them after we cross-dimensionalize."

"Those are your offices," the Weaver explained. "Yes, they are."

"But it's three sizes too big," Nathan whined as he tried to adjust the armor. "And this shield thing weighs a ton." Now Nathan didn't

27

mean to whine. That was just his nature. As sure as Denise had her temper and Josh his ego, Nathan had his whine.

"You will grow into that armor," the Weaver patiently explained. "And the shield will come in most handy."

"Yes, but—"

"This is how he has imaged you, yes, it is. And this is how you will stop the Merchant."

"Merchant?" Nathan asked.

It was Josh's turn to explain. "The Merchant of Emotions. Imager said that—"

"Wait a minute," Nathan interrupted. "You talked to Imager? When?"

"I'll explain later. The point is—"

"I want to know now. When did you talk to—"

"Nathan, for once in your life try not to be the world's biggest brat."

"Who're you calling a—"

"Gentlemen, gentlemen," the Weaver sighed. "I know it's difficult to be civil to each other, but if you will look at these tapestries, you will see we have little time."

The brothers turned back to the tapestries in front of them. Something was wrong. Nathan could see it at once. The intricate beauty of their patterns was . . . disappearing.

Listro Q was the first to speak. "Tapestries, becoming unraveled is their weave."

It was true, each of the tapestries was slowly unraveling. Dozens of beautiful designs were coming undone. The glowing threads were being pulled out of their weave and hanging haphazardly in all directions.

"What's happening?" Josh asked in concern. "They're coming apart."

"An inappropriate observation," Mr. Hornsberry spoke up.

Changes

"Upon closer examination you will note that many of the tapestries are actually reweaving themselves."

The group stepped closer for a better look. It was true. Some of the threads were actually coming together again, intertwining, forming their own patterns. But instead of the beautiful, glowing masterpieces, they were forming gross, clumsy designs.

Samson chattered off a quick question.

The Weaver shook his head and answered, "No, only the tapestries from the Upside-Down Kingdom are being rewoven."

"But . . . why?" Nathan stammered. "Who's responsible?"

The Weaver turned directly to him. He spoke only one word. . . .

"Denise."

The group stood, dumbfounded.

"But how?" Josh finally asked. "How could Denise, how could one person, do all this damage?"

The Weaver looked at him a long moment. Then he turned and stepped forward to one of the tapestries. When he arrived he pushed it aside to reveal a giant, round door. It looked like the door to a bank vault. "Come with me," he said.

The group glanced at one another.

"Where are we going?" Nathan asked.

The Weaver busied himself with dialing a combination in the center of the door, so Aristophenix answered:

> **If I ain't too mistaken,**
> **you'll enjoy this little stroll.**
> **It looks like we're enterin'**
> **someone's Master Control.**

The combination was dialed in. The Weaver pulled on the handle, heaved open the heavy steel door, and stepped into darkness.

With more than a little trepidation, Nathan and the others followed.

□

Denise couldn't believe what she saw as her limo turned into the hospital parking lot. Outside there were hundreds of people. Most were wearing those silly hospital gowns—the type that never quite close in the back. But no one seemed to care. Not anymore. Everyone was too happy and excited.

The limo stopped and Denise threw open the door. Outside everything was chaos and confusion. Everywhere patients were running and leaping and laughing.

"What's going on?" she shouted as she stepped into the mob. "What's happening?"

No one seemed to hear.

"Would somebody please tell me what's going on?"

Finally an old man turned to her. He was very frail and weak. But he was grinning—from ear to ear his toothless gums glistened in the sunlight. "Haven't you heard?" he cackled. "We're healed! There ain't no pain no more!" With that he leaped into the air to click his heels. Of course, he failed miserably and fell to the ground in a crumpled heap. But he didn't care, not in the least—unless you call breaking into uncontrollable laughter "caring."

Denise looked around in disbelief. The place was like a school playground. Old-timers laughed and ran around like children. Pregnant mothers jumped rope. Accident victims played tag. Cancer patients slapped one another on the back, hooting and hollering with joy.

The only ones not smiling were the doctors. "Please, you are not well!" they kept shouting. "You must come back to your rooms."

But no one listened. Why should they? The doctors were obviously wrong. There was no pain. No suffering. Not anymore.

Changes

And Denise knew why. She couldn't help grinning down at the Tablet in her hands. The words NO PAIN were still written in permanent ink upon the stone. *She* had done this. *She, Denise Wolff*, had single-handedly rid the world of pain. With just two words she had erased all of the world's misery and suffering. Her chest swelled with pride and she shook her head in wonder over what she'd so easily accomplished.

She started through the crowd to look for her mom. After all, her mother was the inspiration for all this. "Mom . . . Mom, where are you?"

"Clear the way!" A couple wheelchair patients raced toward her. "Clear the way!" They nearly knocked Denise to the ground as they sped past. "Sorry!" they shouted as they disappeared into the crowd.

"Don't worry," Denise called back. "You couldn't hurt me if you tried!"

She wasn't bragging, just stating a fact. They *couldn't* hurt her. They couldn't hurt *anyone*. She had made the world too good for that. She wasn't sure why Imager had created the mess, but she was sure of one thing . . . with the Tablet, she was going to clean it up. She was going to make everything better, a *lot* better. She gripped the stone more firmly and searched the crowd. "Mom . . ."

"Denny! Denny, over here!"

Denise turned and spotted her mother hobbling through the crowd. Her face was glowing. All trace of suffering was gone. At the moment, she was doing her best to ignore a worried nurse who was pleading with her to sit down.

"Please, Mrs. Wolff, your leg's not ready—"

"Don't be silly. I'm fine."

Denise's grin widened as she pushed through the crowd

toward her mother. She couldn't wait to tell her that she was the one responsible for—

Then Mom came into full view and Denise's joy turned to horror. "Mom, your leg!"

The woman glanced down at her hospital gown. The lower portion was spattered with blood. But it wasn't the blood that concerned Denise. It was the way the leg had turned and twisted in the wrong direction.

"I told her it wasn't healed," the nurse cried as Denise joined them. "I told her it wouldn't hold her weight!"

"Nonsense," Mrs. Wolff laughed. "I feel fine. It doesn't bother me a—"

"But, Mom, it looks awful! And what's this white thing?" Denise bent down for a closer look. She wished she hadn't. The "white thing" was her mother's leg bone! It was still broken, still twisted, and now it jutted through the skin!

"Mom, sit down!"

"Sweetheart, I—"

"*Sit down!*"

Reluctantly her mother let Denise help her to the ground. Then, turning to the crowd, Denise shouted, "Is there a doctor? Please, I need a doctor! I need a doctor here, right away!"

Chapter Five

The Chase Begins

"Wow!" both brothers exclaimed as they entered the large round room. A single desktop circled the entire chamber like a giant ring. Sitting behind the desk, facing the center, were two dozen Fayrahnians. Each carefully studied a little 3-D picture that floated before them. Each carefully adjusted the complex knobs and controls on the desk below those pictures. But that was nothing compared to what floated in the middle of the room.

For there, directly in the center, nearly twenty feet high, was a giant 3-D projection of Denise! She was in a hospital room arguing with two doctors and a nurse over her mother's broken and bleeding leg.

The Weaver quickly explained to the brothers. "Behind each tapestry is a door leading to that person's Master Control."

"You mean each of us has a room like this?" Josh asked.

"Of course."

Josh and Nathan exchanged looks.

"My assistants here carefully monitor the decisions you make in your weave."

"Hold it," Nathan interrupted. "I thought you wove those tapestries the way Imager told you."

"I do."

"Then how—"

"You still have free will. If you refuse Imager's design, you may change it."

"But," Josh argued, "who would want to? I mean, his designs are so incredible."

The Weaver nodded and sighed wearily. "Yours is a most stubborn kingdom, Joshua O'Brien, yes, it is. Many insist on their own weave instead of Imager's." He motioned to the ring desk and continued. "Here we monitor your every decision, down to the tiniest details."

"The details?"

"They are often what change your life the most."

Josh looked at him skeptically.

"Not at first, but five, ten, twenty years into the future. It is the little choices that change your life. The little choices are often—" He was interrupted by a loud, buzzing alarm.

"Sir!" one of the Fayrahnians cried, "we have another Code 12!"

The Weaver quickly crossed to one of the desk stations to study the little 3-D picture floating above it. It was another image of Denise, but in a much different location. "Put it on the big screen!"

The assistant obeyed.

Immediately the big-screen image of Denise in the hospital was replaced by another one. In it she looked awful. She was haggard and very, very frightened. Instead of her usual uniform of baggy pants and T-shirt, she wore some sort of fancy riding outfit. And she carried a large flat stone.

She stood on a beach next to a burning bus. Heading toward her was a mob of people—some crawling, others staggering. But they all had one thing in common: their hatred for Denise. "Nightmare," they shouted. "You've created a nightmare!"

Tears filled Denise's eyes. "No, I . . . I created good!" she shouted. "This is supposed to be good!"

Other voices were heard. "Get the Tablet! Get the Tablet!"

She spun around to see another group—hundreds of them. They were awful to look at. Their bodies were broken and twisted

The Chase Begins

beyond belief. Like the others, they staggered and crawled toward her. "Get the Tablet! Get the Tablet!"

"Monsters!" a third group shouted. "We're all monsters. . . ."

Denise twirled to face them. They were equally as ravaged and twisted.

Filled with panic, she tried to run. But they came at her from every direction. Angry people, broken people, ruined people.

"Nightmare . . ."

They continued to close in.

"Monsters . . ."

They were nearly on top of her.

"Get the Tablet . . ."

"Mr. Hornsberry!" She turned to her companions. "Samson— do something! Help me!"

But there appeared nothing they could do.

Back in Master Control it must have been a shock for Hornsberry and Samson to see themselves up on the projection, but neither spoke a word as they continued watching.

Josh turned to the Weaver and shouted over the noise, "So this is what will happen in the future?"

The Weaver nodded. "*If* she makes the wrong decision in the hospital."

"What's that in her hand?" Nathan yelled. "It looks familiar!"

Aristophenix explained:

The Tablet she has found;
it changes reality.
It's the thing that will bring
all of this calamity.

Joshua turned back to the Weaver for more information.

"This is the future," the Weaver explained. "Yes, it is. This is what will happen if Denise keeps changing Imager's reality."

"It's terrible!" Nathan shouted.

"It is nothing compared to what will follow." The Weaver turned to another assistant. "Punch in thirty seconds beyond what we're viewing."

The assistant obeyed.

The pleading Denise disappeared from the screen and was replaced by another creature. It was large with claws, crystal-clear scales, and huge black leathery wings. Wings that carried it silently through outer space toward a blue, cloud-covered planet that could only be—

"Earth!" Joshua cried. "He's heading for Earth!"

The Weaver nodded sadly.

"That's the Illusionist!" Nathan shouted. "I thought she was dead. I thought we destroyed her."

"Closely, look more," Listro Q called. "The Illusionist is not. Her brother is it."

"Her brother?"

The Weaver explained, "He is called the Merchant of Emotions. He is the creature you must battle, yes, he is. He is the one you must prevent from entering the Upside-Down Kingdom."

"But he's almost there," Joshua cried. "How can we stop—"

"Remember, this is the future you're seeing."

"Yeah, but—"

"Punch up 11–17 Quadrant E," the Weaver ordered.

Another assistant transferred another image to the center screen. It was a kingdom of towering buildings, crowded roadways, and deafening noise. Noise like a thousand stereos blasting at once.

"This is the present time. This is where he has currently

The Chase Begins

landed. He has enslaved this kingdom as he waits to attack yours. You must stop him here."

"But, how?" Joshua demanded. "Imager said something about Nathan's suit of armor and I'm supposed to—"

The Weaver nodded. "Nathan believes in Imager more strongly than you. That armor and shield are his belief, his protection from the Merchant's powers."

"What about me?"

"You are the water bearer. You have Imager's water in that water skin."

Josh instinctively adjusted the water skin around his shoulder that Listro Q had given him.

"Imager's liquid letters and words are your weapons."

"What good is—"

"Nathan told you how the water melted the Kingdom of Seerlo?"

"Well, yes, but—"

"You know how it helps you see as Imager sees?"

"Sure, but—"

"That is only the beginning of its power, yes, it is."

"Hold it," Nathan interrupted. "You're telling us that—"

Suddenly another alarm sounded.

The Weaver spun to the screen. "There's no time to explain!" he shouted. "You must stop the Merchant of Emotions before he reaches your kingdom—before Denise invites him into your world." Turning to Listro he called, "Have you entered their coordinates?"

"Yes, did I."

"Then give him one of the Cross-Dimensionalizers."

Listro Q reached over and handed Nathan the small control unit. "Still remember you, how to use it?"

"Well, yeah, but you guys are coming with."

The Weaver shook his head. "Only the re-Breathed can handle Imager's weapons; only you will be able to stop the Merchant."

"But—"

"Go!"

Again Josh protested, "I still don't see how we can — "

It was Aristophenix's turn for impatience.

> **Don't be a worryin' 'bout it,**
> **we're here watchin' the show.**
> **Just use them gifts wisely,**
> **now hurry and go.**

"Yes, but—"

Another alarm sounded.

"Go!" the Weaver ordered. "Now!"

Joshua looked at his brother.

Nathan took a deep breath, pressed the four buttons on the Cross-Dimensionalizer . . .

BEEP!........BOP!........BLEEP!.......BURP!....

. . . and they were gone.

The Weaver took a deep breath of his own and looked at the rest of the group. "This one's going to be close," he sighed, "yes, it is."

▣

Back in the hospital, Denise clutched the Tablet and shook her head at her mother's doctors—an older gentleman and a younger, good-looking one.

"You don't understand," the older doctor tried to reason. "Pain is good."

The Chase Begins

"No way!" Denise argued. "Pain causes suffering, it causes misery. Everything's better now that I got rid of it!"

"Are you blind?" the younger doctor practically shouted. He pointed to her mom's twisted and bleeding leg. "You call that better? Without pain she doesn't know how badly she was injured. She'll just keep walking on it, making it worse and worse!"

Denise didn't like the young doctor. Not one bit. He was rude and arrogant. "You're telling me that we *need* pain?" she scorned.

"Yes," the older doctor insisted. "It's nature's way of saying something's wrong."

"You're crazy. I destroyed pain to make the world a better place!"

"You're wrong!" the younger doctor exploded.

"And you're jealous!" she shouted back. "Because me and this Tablet here, we just put you two out of business!"

"That's not it!" he insisted. "That's not it at all!" He raced to the window. "Look!" Before anyone could stop him, he leaned back and smashed his hand through the glass of the upper window.

"Doctor!" the older physician cried out.

But he paid no attention. Instead, he held out his bleeding hand to her. "Look! No pain!" He spun around and smashed it through the lower window.

"Doctor!"

Again he held it out. Only now it was in much worse shape. "Don't you see?" he pleaded. "I could do this all day and it wouldn't matter. I could get sick, burn myself, get hit by a truck—without pain I'd never know I needed help. Without pain I'd eventually kill myself!"

But Denise had made the world a better place. She wasn't about to let some doctor convince her to change it back. "No!" she insisted. "I made things better, and that's how they're going to stay!"

"We'll see about that," the younger doctor sneered. Suddenly he lunged for the Tablet.

Denise screamed and jumped back.

"Get the Tablet!" he shouted.

The older doctor and the nurse joined in. Soon they had Denise pinned against the wall as they tried to rip the Tablet from her.

"Stop it!" Denise's mom yelled as she hobbled into the fight. "Stop it!"

Denise continued screaming but it did no good. Hands came at her from all sides. She dropped to the floor and wrapped herself around the stone. She began kicking and biting—anything to keep them away.

Then she saw it. Between their legs. An opening. And past that, the door. She scampered between the legs and leaped up. In an instant she was out the door and in the hallway.

"Stop her! Stop her!"

She sprinted down the hall and knocked a couple patients off their feet. But it didn't matter. Since they didn't feel pain, they just sat there laughing.

She came to the end of the hall, looked in both directions, and darted to the right. She wasn't sure where she was going, but she could hear the younger doctor closing in from behind.

"Stop!" he ordered. "Stop!"

No way.

An open doorway came into view. She dashed into the room and tried to slam the door and lock it. But the younger doctor was too fast. Before she could get it closed, he was pushing against it. She pushed back as hard as she could, but he continued to shove it forward inch by inch.

"Denise . . . please . . . be reasonable."

The Chase Begins

She was losing ground. Any second he'd be inside. Suddenly she had an idea. If the Tablet could do anything, then maybe . . .

She pulled up the Tablet and fumbled for the marker.

"Denise . . ."

The door was nearly open. Already his arm and shoulder were squeezing in. Already he was reaching toward her.

Furiously, she scrawled the letters with the felt pen until she finally completed the words: *OBEY ME!*

But nothing happened! The doctor just kept coming! With a final push, he shoved through and grabbed her! She screamed, but it did no good. Why? What was wrong?

"Okay," he panted, "it's over. Give it to me." He held out his hand, waiting.

Denise's mind raced. *Why didn't the Tablet work?*

He grabbed the Tablet, but she still wouldn't let go. "All right, if that's the way you want it." He started prying her fingers loose—one at a time.

Suddenly she had it. Of course! He hadn't obeyed her because she hadn't given him an order!

The Tablet was nearly in his hands. Just two more fingers to go. "Be a good girl now and let—"

"Stop it!" Denise commanded.

Immediately the doctor stopped. A look of confusion crossed his face. Finally he spoke. "I'm . . . I'm sorry, Ms. Wolff . . . I don't know what came over me."

Denise watched him cautiously.

"I do hope you'll forgive me. May I walk you back to your mother's room?"

Denise hesitated, then slowly answered, "Sure." Just to be safe she pulled the Tablet in a bit closer.

The doctor held open the door for her and they entered the hallway.

Denise still wasn't a hundred percent sure. Was he just faking it or had the Tablet really worked? And if it worked, did that mean that no matter what she asked, he would have to obey her? She hated to do it, but there was really only one way to find out.

"Excuse me, Doctor?"

"Yes."

"Would you bark like a dog for me, please?"

The man instantly dropped to his knees and began to bark.

Everyone in the hall stared in amazement. Everyone but Denise. "Thank you, Doctor," she said with a contented smile, "thank you very much."

Chapter Six

And Now, for Your Entertainment

At first Joshua thought they'd cross-dimensionalized back home. This new kingdom looked exactly like any major city in any major country. Towering buildings, masses of people, and traffic backed up for blocks. But it didn't take long to see that things were just a little bit different. . . .

First there was the noise. Deafening. Like a thousand stereos and TVs all blaring at the same time.

Then there were the windows. Actually the lack of them. In place of windows there were . . . movie screens. That's right. Whether they were the windows in cars, or the thousands of windows in a skyscraper, or the huge display windows of a department store, every pane of glass had been replaced by a motion picture screen. And every screen was playing a different movie! It was impossible to look anywhere without seeing at least twenty movies playing at the same time.

As a result, the people on the street barely moved. Why should they? What was happening on those screens, what filled their vision and blasted into their ears was a thousand times more interesting than real life. So they simply stood and stared

"What is this place?" Nathan shouted.

But Joshua barely heard. The noise was too deafening. Not far away, he spotted a lone woman in rags. She seemed to be the only one moving as she pushed a rusty shopping cart down the street. He headed for her, with Nathan at his side.

"Excuse me, ma'am!" he shouted. "Ma'am, could you tell us where we are?"

"The Kingdom of Entertainment!" she shouted back.

"I'm sorry, I can barely hear you!"

"THE KINGDOM OF ENTERTAINMENT!"

Josh looked at his brother, still not entirely sure he understood.

The woman reached into her cart and brought out two sets of clear little balls, just slightly larger than marbles. She handed a pair to each boy and motioned for them to put them in their ears. Figuring he had nothing to lose, Josh popped them inside. So did his brother. And suddenly he heard . . .

Silence.

Beautiful, blessed silence.

"That will be 2,340 jairkens," the woman said, holding out her hand for payment.

Josh and Nathan traded looks. "I'm sorry," Nathan answered. "We don't have any of those . . . 'jairken' things."

"No jairkens!" she scorned. "Then give those back before I call the enforcers!"

"But," Josh protested, "without them it's so noisy we won't be able to hear ourselves think."

"That's the whole idea!" a voice boomed from behind.

The brothers spun around to see the same black-winged creature they'd viewed in Denise's Master Control. Its image was projected upon the glass panes of a revolving hotel door and it flickered as the panes spun around. Hiding behind it was the image of a large, eight-legged type of dog—frightened, but obviously trying to sneak a peek at them.

"It's the Merchant of Emotions," Nathan shouted to his brother.

"Very good." The Merchant grinned. "So tell me"—he gave a sweeping gesture with one of his claws—"what do you think of my world?"

And Now, for Your Entertainment

"Your world?" Joshua asked.

"Well, it is now that they've made me their god."

"Why would they do that?" Nathan demanded.

The Merchant shrugged. "Appreciation, I suppose. All these people you see here wanted to be entertained. So I gave them exactly what they wanted."

"Which was . . . ?" Josh asked.

"Entertainment." He broke into a brief cackle. "Nonstop, never-ceasing entertainment. Now they'll never be able to hear themselves think. Most importantly, they'll never again be able to hear Imager's wretched voice. Their only relief is in buying silence—and that, my little friends, costs a pretty jairken."

"I should say so," the street vendor complained. "And they've just stolen four minutes' worth."

"Put it on my tab." The Merchant smiled.

"You have no tab," she argued. "And if I keep giving away silence I'll be as poor as a—"

Before she could finish, the Merchant reached for the machine strapped to his chest and flipped a single switch. A cloud of mist shot from a little nozzle and gently settled upon her stomach. Suddenly, she began to cry. Uncontrollably. Deep, gut-wrenching sobs that shook her entire body.

The brothers looked on in astonishment as she dropped to her knees and continued to weep.

"What did you do to her?" Joshua shouted.

"Oh, she's just feeling a little *sentimental*."

"But . . . how?" Nathan stammered.

The creature grinned and gave the nozzle a small pat. "Just my little Emotion Generator."

"You mean you can control—"

"People's emotions?" the Merchant yawned. "Yes, that certainly appears to be the case, doesn't it? Would you care for a demonstration?"

"No!" Josh and Nathan shouted in unison.

"Yes, well, we'll see." The Merchant smiled as he carefully looked them over. "So, Imager has sent you two worthless creatures to try and stop my attack upon his Upside-Down Kingdom."

"We're not worthless," Josh said, taking half a step closer. "We've been re-Breathed and we have our weapons."

"Yes, a bag of water and a rather ill-fitting suit of armor."

Nathan shifted uncomfortably.

"You must remind me to give you the name of my tailor. He could do wonders."

Josh had had enough. If they were to stop this Merchant thing, then they would stop him. He started toward the revolving doors.

"Joshua!" Nathan shouted.

"Don't worry, he's just a reflection."

"Tell that to her," Nathan motioned to the old lady still crying on the sidewalk.

But Josh continued forward. He always had plenty of confidence in whatever he did. Why should this be any different?

"My, my, my, will you look at that, TeeBolt," the Merchant chuckled to the animal still hiding behind his legs. "The Josh is a brave one, isn't he?"

The animal whined and thumped its tail.

Joshua called back to Nathan. "Come on, we can take him." As he approached, he reached down and unscrewed the cap to his water skin. He wasn't exactly sure what he was going to do when he got there, but since the water was all he had and since it had proved its power in the past . . .

"The Josh has bravery," the Merchant said. "Shall we see if he has anything else?" He quickly reached to his Emotion Generator.

"Josh!" Nathan cried. "Look out!"

The Merchant flipped another switch. A thin mist shot out and struck Josh on the right side of the head.

Suddenly, Joshua began screaming in terror.

"Josh!" Nathan raced to him. "Josh, what is it?"

But Joshua couldn't speak. He was too terrified. All he could do was point down at the sidewalk and scream.

"Josh!"

Again he pointed—urgently, desperately—screaming for all he was worth.

"I don't understand! What is it?"

Joshua was beside himself. Why couldn't Nathan see it? It was right there on the sidewalk! Monstrous! Horrifying! An ant! And it was crawling straight toward him! Finally, in desperation, he raced to the nearby wall and cowered against it, whimpering and shaking like a leaf. Wouldn't somebody save him?

"Stop it!" Nathan yelled at the Merchant. "Whatever . . . doing . . . him . . . you better . . . now!"

Josh strained to hear the words but the kingdom's noise was returning. He turned toward the Merchant to see him laughing. When he spoke, Josh could only make out part of his sentence.

"You . . . no match . . . ha, ha, ha . . . will suffer . . . !"

Apparently, the marbles in Josh's ears were losing power. So he did the only thing he could do . . . he screamed louder and shook harder. Then he saw the Merchant reaching for another switch on his Emotion Generator and pointing the nozzle at Nathan. . . .

᛭

After a few more barks and a long howl, the young doctor hopped back to his feet and continued down the hall with Denise. She could tell that he was embarrassed, but she had given him an order and, well, she was the boss. To have that much control felt good and, she had to admit, a little dizzying. Because she wasn't just the boss over the doctor. With the Tablet she was the boss over everybody. Now she had absolute power. Not that she ever planned to misuse it. But still, to have so much of it . . .

The elevator doors opened and two orderlies rushed out carrying an old man—the same one Denise had met when she stepped out of the limo—the same toothless gentleman who had jumped up and tried to click his heels. Only now he wasn't jumping. He wasn't even breathing.

Immediately the doctor was at his side. "What's wrong?"

"Heart attack!" one of the orderlies shouted.

"Set him down," the doctor ordered. "Get a crash cart, stat! We have a code blue!"

"The crash carts are all busy," the second orderly cried. "People are dropping like flies out there—everyone's overdoing it; they're all killing themselves!"

Without a word the doctor dropped to his knees and began pumping the old man's chest. Then he pinched the man's nose and began breathing into his mouth.

"What's happening?" Denise cried. "What's going on?"

"Without pain, no one knows their limits," the doctor explained as he turned from the man's mouth and began pumping his chest again. "Without pain, everyone will die."

The thought caught Denise off guard—but only for a second. If that was the only problem . . . and if she could control anything.

And Now, for Your Entertainment

. . Quickly she raised the Tablet and scrawled out two more words with her marker: *NO DEATH*.

Suddenly the old man came back to life—coughing, wheezing, and looking around very wide-eyed. But he was alive, there was no doubt about it.

The doctor stared up at Denise, his own eyes widening in astonishment.

"Well," Denise grinned, "that should take care of that."

◙

Back in Master Control another alarm sounded.

Aristophenix, Listro Q, Samson, and Mr. Hornsberry had all been watching Denise on the main screen. And they all had cringed when she made the doctor bark like a dog. But now she was back to using the Tablet for good. Now things were getting better. Or so they thought.

"Alarm, what for?" Listro Q asked. "By eliminating death, didn't a good thing do she?"

The Weaver shook his head angrily. "Punch up the future!" he shouted to an assistant. "Punch up three hundred years into the future."

The big screen flickered. Now they stared at an incredibly old and outrageously fat queen. In fact, she was so huge that it took three thrones just to hold her. With all the wrinkles and rolls of fat, it was hard to recognize the face. But since this was Denise's Control Room, and since they were watching Denise, everyone had a pretty good idea who it was. She was so old and so fat that she couldn't move. And yet she was sighing in pleasure. Incredible, indescribable pleasure. The reason soon became apparent. The Merchant of Emotions was standing right beside her . . . covering her with thick mists of his emotions.

"Pull back!" the Weaver called.

The image pulled back to show more of the scene. Now they could see Denise's thrones were in the middle of a desert—an endless desert surrounded by thick, putrid air. Air so dark that it was impossible to tell whether it was day or night. Millions of people were crowded around her, coughing and choking, trying to breathe but finding it impossible.

Samson chattered a question.

The Weaver answered, "Without death, Upside Downers will overrun their kingdom and use up all its resources."

It was true. There were no trees or grass or even oceans—just people, billions and billions of swarming people. "Swarming" probably isn't the right word because to swarm you have to move. These people were so crowded together that they couldn't move. All they could do was cough and choke . . . and plead.

"Please," they begged the gigantic Denise. "Please let us die. Have mercy on us, please let us die, please . . ."

It appeared their bodies had simply worn out. Those who still had arms and legs could no longer use them. Yet, they could not die. They were forced to live century after century like this.

Still, they had no physical pain. How could they? That had been Denise's first order. But there appeared to be a different type of pain. A pain of the mind. A torture of having to live hundreds of years. A torture of having to survive in this harsh, impossibly crowded world. A torture of knowing things would only grow worse.

Aristophenix turned to the Weaver.

> You'll have to excuse me,
> I'm usually quite clever.
> But is this what happens
> when Upside Downers live forever?

And Now, for Your Entertainment

The Weaver slowly nodded. "In the beginning, when Upside Downers turned from Imager, he commanded me to weave Death into their world."

"This, because of?" Listro Q asked, motioning toward the screen.

Again the Weaver nodded. "To live forever in any kingdom without Imager is impossibly cruel. Without Imager's rule, death is a gift, not a curse. Without Imager, death is mercy."

"But"—Mr. Hornsberry cleared his throat—"why is Denise so phenomenally overweight and insensitive?"

"She's done away with all of life's struggles, yes, she has," the Weaver answered. "Without struggles and hardships she has grown fat and lazy."

"Laziness of her body," Listro Q commented.

"And of her mind," Aristophenix added.

"And most dangerous of all," the Weaver continued, "there is a fatness to her soul, a laziness of her spirit."

The group stood looking on in silence.

"Still," Mr. Hornsberry asked, "this is not necessarily the future. If Master Nathan and Joshua are successful in their attempts to stop the Merchant, this will all change."

The Weaver nodded. "*If* they can stop him."

Silence again settled over the group. Only the choking and moaning from the screen filled the room.

Finally, the Weaver could stand no more. "Go back to the present," he ordered. Once again the projected image flickered and changed.

Samson began to chatter.

"Yes," the Weaver agreed, "in case Joshua and Nathan fail, a back-up plan would be good."

Again Samson spoke.

Again the Weaver agreed. "Because of your closeness to her, she *might* listen. But the risk of a non-Upside Downer in this sort of situation is—"

Samson cut him off with another burst of chatter.

"I appreciate your devotion, but even if you did go, she still doesn't understand your language. She'd need a translator."

"Us have you," Listro Q offered.

The Weaver shook his head. "No, the risk of more than one non-Upside Downer there is too great."

The group stood a moment watching.

Again Listro Q spoke. "But, if somebody else from the Upside-Down Kingdom find could we—" His eyes turned to Mr. Hornsberry.

The dog shifted uncomfortably. "Did I miss something?"

"From the Upside-Down Kingdom, need we someone."

"Yes." The dog cleared his throat. "And your point is . . ."

Aristophenix turned toward Hornsberry, also seeing it. "Of course, someone of great courage . . ."

The Weaver nodded and joined in. "Someone of great intelligence . . ."

"And wisdom have must he," Listro Q added.

"Absolutely," Aristophenix agreed. Then, smiling at Mr. Hornsberry he asked, "Now, who do you suppose that special someone could be?"

Mr. Hornsberry swallowed nervously. As he was the only other citizen from the Upside-Down Kingdom, there was little doubt who they were referring to.

"I would be happy to volunteer," he coughed slightly, "most happy, indeed. However, if you recall, back home I am merely a

And Now, for Your Entertainment

stuffed animal. If you return me to the Upside-Down Kingdom, I'm afraid I shall once again become—"

"I could adjust your weave," the Weaver offered. "Temporarily, you understand."

"That would be most considerate, however . . ."

The group waited in hopeful anticipation.

"That is to say . . ."

They continued to wait.

Mr. Hornsberry gave another nervous cough.

They waited some more.

"Oh, very well," he sighed. "If anyone was created to save the day, I suppose it is myself."

"All right, Mr. Hornsberry!" The group cheered and slapped him on the back.

"What a guy!" Aristophenix said.

"A hero is he," Listro Q agreed.

"Yes, well," Mr. Hornsberry cleared his throat, "that goes without saying now, doesn't it."

"You'll need this." The Weaver suddenly and quite mysteriously produced another Cross-Dimensionalizer.

Mr. Hornsberry gave him a look. "You perceived that I would accompany Samson all along, didn't you?"

The Weaver gave the slightest shrug. "I am the Weaver, yes, I am." Then, without hesitating, he continued with further instruction. "Now, you must do your best to convince Denise to destroy the Tablet. And she must return everything to the original weave. Do you understand?"

Samson and Mr. Hornsberry nodded.

Without another word (and obviously fearful Hornsberry would change his mind,) the Weaver stooped down and hung the

Cross-Dimensionalizer around the dog's neck. Then he quickly
punched the four buttons . . .

BEEP!........BOP!........BLEEP!.......BURP!....

. . . and they were gone.

Chapter Seven

A Close Call

"I say, this is rather odd!" Mr. Hornsberry exclaimed as he looked around the enormous room with its towering pillars, full-length windows, and sparkling chandeliers. "Do you have the slightest idea where we might be?"

Samson fired back a reply. It was long and loud. But no matter how long or loud, the answer was still your basic . . . "Nope."

Mr. Hornsberry started to trot around the room, carefully investigating. "Apparently it is some sort of mansion—a palace by all appearances. Yet, what would Denise be doing in such a residence? And what is that irritating ruckus outside?"

Beyond the windows they could hear an angry crowd shouting and yelling. Before they could look further, a large door at the far end of the room opened and a tall, stuffy butler appeared. He was stiff, and, if possible, even more snooty than Mr. Hornsberry. "May I help you?" he inquired.

Realizing the man's attempt at being a snob, Mr. Hornsberry rose to the occasion and tried to out do him. "That is your reason for employment, is it not? Now, be a good fellow and run along to fetch Miss Denise, Wolff. We'd like a word with her."

"I beg your pardon, but whom, or shall I say, *what* is calling?"

The butler was better than Mr. Hornsberry had thought. But that was okay, it would be nice to have a little competition for a change. Before he could return an appropriate insult, Samson started to buzz the man's head.

The butler appeared unfazed. Instead, he simply turned for the door.

"I don't believe you've been dismissed," Mr. Hornsberry called.

"Actually," the butler answered as he tried to swat Samson aside, "I was about to procure some bug spray."

Little Samson squealed in panic.

"No way!" Mr. Hornsberry cried. Then catching himself, he continued with a bit more sophistication. "That is to say, I see no purpose in implementing such barbaric actions."

"And while I'm at it, I think I shall call the dog pound. Talking animals can be such a nuisance."

"You'll do nothing of the kind." Denise appeared at the door behind the butler. Instead of her usual baggy pants and sweatshirt, she was decked out in a riding habit complete with riding whip and derby. She continued. "These folks are my friends and you will treat them with the respect they deserve."

"Miss Denise," Hornsberry shouted. He quickly trotted toward her, careful to turn up his nose while passing the butler.

Denise turned to the man. "That will be all, Chauncey."

"As you wish, ma'am." The butler turned to exit. As he did he fired off one last comment to Mr. Hornsberry. "Try not to shed on the furniture. Dog hair can be so loathsome."

For the briefest second Hornsberry wanted to sink his teeth deep into the man's calf. The fellow wanted loathsome, he'd show him loathsome. But somehow he was able to resist the temptation. After all, he did have a reputation to uphold.

Meanwhile, Samson, who was also excited to see Denise, began playfully dive-bombing her head.

"Hey, fella!" she giggled, trying to fight him off. "Cut it out. Come on now," she laughed, "stop it."

And, just that fast, Samson fell to the ground, unable to fly.

"Sammy!" Denise dropped to her knees. "Are you okay?"

A Close Call

"What happened?" Mr. Hornsberry cried.

"I don't know, I just . . . Oh, of course, I get it."

"Get what?"

"Well, I have this thing to write on." She held up the Tablet. "And whatever I write on it happens."

"Yes, we're well aware of that fact."

"Well, one of the things I wrote was that people have to obey me."

"I fail to see how—"

"I told Sammy to stop bothering me, and he had to stop."

Samson chattered a terse reply.

"Sorry, little guy," Denise said sympathetically, "but around here, I'm kinda like the boss. However . . ." she said, pretending to sound very official, "you hereby have my permission to fly again."

Samson took off and began giving Denise the lecture of her life, though this time he was careful to keep his distance.

Mr. Hornsberry didn't bother to translate. He figured Denise would catch the general drift. Instead, he had a few questions of his own. "Would you mind telling me why you are wearing such costly clothes?"

"Oh," Denise laughed, giving her riding whip a couple of slaps against her leg. "I saw this in a magazine and it was so expensive I figured I'd give it a try. You know, to see what the big deal was. When you can have anything you want, it's kinda hard not to go for the best."

"Yes, well, I'm afraid that's one of the reasons the Weaver has sent us."

"The Weaver sent you?" Denise asked. "Cool!"

"He knows all about the Tablet."

"So he's sent you guys to thank me for helping out?"

"Well, not exact—"

"I know these clothes and this palace are no big deal—anybody could wish for them. But it took some real thinking to figure how to make the world better for everybody."

Samson chattered off a sharp reply.

Mr. Hornsberry carefully translated, "Actually, in your admirable efforts to transform the world to a superior status, it appears you are actually destroying it."

Denise's mouth dropped. "I'm what?"

Mr. Hornsberry coughed slightly. "Destroying it."

"No way," she argued. "I'm making this place *better*. A lot better!"

Samson chattered his most stinging comment yet.

"Sure I am," Denise argued, not waiting for the translation. "'Course, not everyone understands it's for the best, but they will."

"Not everyone?" Mr. Hornsberry asked.

She nodded somewhat sadly, then motioned toward the balcony doors. "Don't you hear all that shouting and screaming outside?"

"That is directed toward you?"

"I'm afraid so." She crossed to the giant pair of doors. As she threw them open, the shouting and screaming grew louder.

"They want me to bring pain back into the world." She shook her head. "Can you believe it?"

Mr. Hornsberry and Samson moved to the balcony for a better look. Below them were hundreds of people—all shaking their fists and yelling. And for good reason. Their bodies were twisted and disfigured beyond belief. Many were doubled over with disease or sprawled out on the lawn unable to walk. Several looked as if they should have been dead. But, of course, in Denise's new world, that was no longer possible.

"A few even want me to bring death back." She sighed heavily. "They just don't get it."

A Close Call

"But my dear Denise. Pain and death . . . they're all part of Imager's plan. Can you not see how you are disrupting his Tapestries?"

"Disrupting?" Denise bristled. "I'm not disrupting anything. I'm only making things better."

Samson darted back and forth, speaking angrily.

Mr. Hornsberry translated. "Imager knows what's best. You've ignored his plans and changed the rules."

"No." She shook her head. "I've just added a few of my own to fix things up."

"And *your* rules," Mr. Hornsberry asked, referring to the shouting mob below, "you are certain they are 'fixing things up'?"

Denise stared down at the shouting crowd. "Hmm . . ." She tapped her foot, obviously thinking. "You know . . . you just might be on to something."

Mr. Hornsberry glanced at Samson in smug satisfaction. He'd been there less than five minutes and he was already solving the crisis.

"Yes," Denise said, beginning to nod. "That's my problem. You're right, there *are* too many rules."

"I beg your pardon?" Mr. Hornsberry asked.

She continued. "Not only do they have to follow all of Imager's rules, but they also have to follow mine. Of course. That's why they're so unhappy . . . there's way too many rules to follow."

"Miss Denise—" Hornsberry nervously cleared his throat.

"No one's really let them do what *they* want to do."

"Miss Denise—"

"If you really want people to be happy, you got to give them freedom." She broke into a grin. "Of course! Mr. Hornsberry, you're a genius!"

Hornsberry gave a shiver of delight in spite of himself. "How exactly has my intellect been of service?"

But Denise was no longer listening. Instead, she picked up the Tablet and pen and prepared to write.

"What are you doing?" Hornsberry asked.

Samson hovered over her shoulder for a closer look.

"Imager's got all these rules, right? *Do this, don't do that*. No wonder nobody's happy. What do we need all the rules for?"

Before Hornsberry could respond, she answered, "We don't. To really be happy we need to be free." She wrote on the Tablet as she continued speaking. "We should do only what *we* want to do. Live only the way *we* want to live."

She finished writing and flipped the board around for them to see. There were only two words: *NO RULES*.

Immediately, people below the balcony started screaming. "Get her! Get the Tablet! Get the Tablet!" Soon, the entire crowd joined in, "GET THE TABLET . . . GET THE TABLET!"

They began banging on the door below. "GET THE TABLET . . . GET THE TABLET . . ."

"Stop it!" Denise yelled down to them. "I command you to stop!"

But they continued pounding on the door. "GET THE TABLET . . . GET THE TABLET . . ."

"I thought they had to obey you!" Mr. Hornsberry yelled.

"They do!" She shouted. "I don't understand why—" Suddenly she broke into a sheepish grin.

"What?" Hornsberry shouted.

"GET THE TABLET . . . GET THE TABLET . . ."

"I just wrote that there are no rules, right?"

"That is correct."

A Close Call

"So now they don't have to obey me; now they don't have to obey anyone!"

"GET THE TABLET . . . GET THE TABLET . . ."

"If that's the case," Mr. Hornsberry shouted, "might I inquire if you have an alternate exit?"

"Sure," she yelled. "Why?"

"GET THE TABLET . . . GET THE TABLET . . ." Suddenly the crowd broke through the front doors, swarmed into the mansion, and started up the stairs.

Hornsberry shouted his answer. "So we may make a hasty retreat!"

▣

In the Kingdom of Entertainment the Merchant's image still flickered in the revolving door, and Joshua still cowered against the building.

"Joshua!" Nathan shouted. "Joshua, can you hear me?"

But Joshua was too busy screaming to hear anything.

Nathan twirled back to the Merchant. "What was that? What did you hit him with?"

"Why, isn't it obvious?" the Merchant chuckled. "I just shared a little bit of *terror* with him."

Only then did Nathan see the Merchant had pointed the nozzle at him. Before he could move, the Merchant flipped another switch and another cloud of vapor shot from his Emotion Generator. Nathan tried to raise his shield and block the mist, but he was too late. It hit him dead center in the chest.

Yet nothing happened. Unlike Joshua, or the silence peddler who was still on her knees sobbing, there was no uncontrollable feeling. No all-consuming emotion.

Puzzled, Nathan looked down. Sure enough, there was the

mist. It rested right there on his breastplate. So why had nothing happened? And then he realized the mist hadn't reached his body because of the armor. That clunky armor he hauled around had finally served a purpose. But not for long. For even as he watched, he could see the tiny droplets of moisture eating through the metal, turning it to a liquid goo, working its way closer and closer to his skin.

He spun back to his brother. "Joshua! Joshua, can you hear me?"

But Joshua was too busy screaming. At least he looked like he was screaming. Nathan could no longer hear. His marbles of silence were wearing off. The roar of the kingdom's speakers and movie screens filled his head.

The Merchant fired off another cloud of mist. This time Nathan was fast enough to block it with his shield. But when the mist hit, the shield itself started to dissolve. Nathan had no alternative but to turn and start running. But not away. No, he would not desert his brother. Instead, he ran to the silence peddler's cart and grabbed four more marbles. He quickly slipped two into his ears and rushed back to Josh with the other pair.

"What are you doing?" the Merchant cried. He reached down to his Generator and fired off two more clouds of mist. Nathan was so busy helping his brother that he didn't have time to raise his shield and defend himself. Both volleys hit him on the armor of his right leg.

But Nathan wasn't concerned about those hits. He was concerned about the first one. The one whose mist had finally eaten through his breastplate. Already he could feel its wetness touching his skin—and with that wetness came an uncontrollable emotion . . . *worry*. Worry about everything: Joshua, Denise, friends, school . . . he even began to worry about worrying. He knew it

A Close Call

wasn't real. He knew it all came from the Merchant. But he also knew there was nothing he could do to stop it.

He dropped to his knees. "This is not happening!" he cried.

The Merchant of Emotions laughed. "You think that's something—wait until those other emotions eat their way through to you!"

Frantically Nathan looked at his right leg armor. The other emotions were quickly dissolving the metal just as the first one had.

"No!" he cried, fighting against the *worry*. "Nooo!"

The Merchant continued laughing.

"No! No! No!" Nathan screamed, but it did no good. The emotion was too strong to fight. In a final, desperate act, he cried, "Imager promised we would win! Imager promised!"

And with that cry, the strangest thing happened . . .

As Nathan shouted, as he declared Imager's promise, the mist of *worry* began to evaporate. Nathan could actually feel the dampness start to leave his chest. And, as it left, so did the *worry*.

Amazed, he shouted again. "Imager promised! We'll win! *We will win!*"

To his astonishment, not only did the moisture evaporate from his chest but the hole in his breastplate began to seal. The metal was actually sealing itself, becoming as smooth and shiny as if it had never been pierced. He looked down at his right leg armor. The same was happening there. He looked at his shield for the earlier hit. The same thing.

What had the Weaver said . . . "*The armor and shield are your belief—your protection.*" Of course, that was it! They were his belief! They were his trust in Imager! Somehow as he held on to Imager's promise, he had activated their power.

Now the armor was as good as new. Slowly, with greater resolve, Nathan rose to his feet and turned to face the Merchant.

He wasn't crazy about it, but by the looks of things, it was time for a little showdown.

Quickly, the Merchant fired off another round of emotion. And then another. But Nathan blocked each one with his shield. As they struck the metal, they spattered loudly and evaporated with a hiss.

"What has the Nathan done?" the Merchant shouted. "What has he done to my emotions?"

Nathan turned back to his brother, who was still screaming in *terror*. He'd already shoved the marbles of silence into his ears but it did nothing to stop the fear. "Josh!" he shouted. "Josh, you've got to listen to me!"

But Joshua was still overwhelmed.

What could he do? And then he spotted it. The mist the Merchant had fired at his brother. It was still on the side of his head, still glistening in the blue-green light of the surrounding TV screens.

Nathan reached out his armored glove to it. Ever so gently he touched the moisture. It spattered and hissed viciously.

Josh blinked.

Nathan touched some more. And every place he touched, the moisture evaporated . . . until it had completely disappeared.

Josh blinked again, then shook his head, trying to get his bearings. "What . . . what happened?" he asked.

Nathan leaned closer and looked into his eyes. As best he could tell the *terror* his brother had been experiencing was gone.

"What happened?" Josh repeated.

"It's the Merchant," Nathan said, pointing toward the revolving doors. "He was controlling you with—"

But when Nathan turned he saw the Merchant was no longer there. He had disappeared.

A Close Call

"Look!" Josh shouted, struggling to his feet. He pointed to the windows of the hotel, then to other buildings. "The TV and movie screens—they're gone. All of them! They're all glass again!"

"And the noise," Nathan said. He pulled the marbles from his ears to make sure. "It's also gone!"

It's true. Things were peaceful and quiet. Well, as peaceful and quiet as any big city can be . . . if you don't count the honking horns, squealing brakes, and screaming people.

"Do you see him?" Josh asked, looking around.

Nathan shook his head. "He's not here. He must have left."

"Good."

Nathan agreed. "At least for the people of this kingdom."

"So where do you think he'd go? I mean after he left this kingdom where would he . . ." Josh came to a stop. He turned to Nathan, his eyes widening in concern. "Quick, the Cross-Dimensionalizer!"

Immediately Nathan understood. He pulled the Cross-Dimensionalizer from his pocket and shouted into it. "Listro Q! Listro Q, you have to get us to Earth—*now!*"

The unit crackled to life. "At your home, he is not. One more kingdom, visiting first is he."

"Then send us there—we have to stop him!"

"Entering the coordinates now am I."

The brothers exchanged looks. In learning how to fight the Merchant, they'd nearly lost the first battle. Hopefully they'd be ready for the next.

"Ready!" Listro Q shouted.

Nathan nodded and reached down to press the buttons.

BEEP!........BOP!........BLEEP!........BURP!....

Chapter Eight

The Out-of-Timers

"*Now* where are we?" Josh asked.

Nathan shook his head. At first glance it looked like some kind of overgrown park. But a very weird overgrown park. There were lots of trees, yet they were all perfectly straight and had no branches. They were planted in single file and covered with ivy. Below them were wide, overgrown paths of concrete that stretched as far as the eye could see. And on those paths were . . . could it be? Yes. They were cars—broken-down, rusted-out cars. Hundreds of them. Which meant those concrete lanes weren't pathways at all, but overgrown streets. And the branchless trees in straight lines? What else but telephone poles!

Then there were the people . . .

Nathan saw them sitting inside the cars and on top of them chatting away. Like the cars and the rest of the kingdom, they were dirty and broken down—hair messed, faces unshaven, sporting the latest fashion in worn and tattered clothing.

Then there was the smell. *Their* smell. It was so strong that it made Nathan's nose tickle. It was a safe bet that soap and water weren't something this kingdom had discovered yet. Or if it had, then like the streets, cars, and telephone poles, its citizens simply didn't care enough to use them.

And, speaking of "not caring," no one seemed too surprised when the brothers suddenly cross-dimensionalized in front of them.

"Excuse me," Josh called to a nearby car. Its doors had rusted

The Out-of-Timers

off and it was filled with a handful of elderly people. "Excuse me, could you tell us where we are?"

At first no one bothered to answer. They just continued their conversation.

"Excuse me!"

Finally a ragged, white-haired man from the front seat shouted, "We can't tell you where you *are*, but we can tell you where you *arrived*."

Nathan threw a look at Josh. "I'm sorry, what?"

"We were Out-of-Timers."

"*Out-of-Timers?*" Josh asked.

"That *was* correct. We *were* Out-of-Timers."

Again the brothers traded glances. "What do you mean, *were*?" Nathan asked. "What are you now?"

"We had no *now*. Nor will we have one in the future."

"What?" Josh exclaimed.

"What do you mean, you have no now?" Nathan asked.

The man turned to the group in the backseat. "I had forgotten how stupid youth was." The others chuckled and clucked their tongues in agreement. The white-haired man turned back to Joshua. "We neither had a *now* in the past nor will we have a *now* in the future. We will think only of our past or of our future. We have not lived nor will we ever live in the *now*."

Nathan turned to his brother. "You're the brain. What's he saying?"

"I'm not sure," Josh scowled. "But I think he's saying these people don't have a *present*."

"What?"

"It sounds like they can remember the past okay. And they can think about the future . . . but they don't have a *now*."

"They don't have a *now*?" Nathan repeated.

Josh nodded. "They can't enjoy the present."

"That's awful!"

"It *was* awful," the white-haired man agreed. "And it *will be* awful."

"Is that why everything is falling apart?" Nathan asked. "Because there is no *now* for you to fix things up?"

"We *have* fixed things and we *will* fix things, but we can't fix things now because—"

"—there is no *now*," Josh cut in impatiently, "yeah, I got it. But who is responsible for this?"

"There never was an *is* nor will there be an *is*."

"All right, all right, who *was* responsible for this?"

A beggar from the backseat spoke up. "The creature with the eight-legged pet—the creature with all the emotions had returned to us."

"The Merchant!" Nathan gasped.

"He'd been here before?" Josh asked.

"Yes, many times."

"And he's here now?"

"He *was* here. And he *will be* here, but—"

"I know, I know," Nathan sighed, "but there is no *now* so he's not here."

The beggar nodded with satisfaction. The group turned to one another and resumed speaking of the past, recalling how the Merchant had cast his spell—how he had stolen their *now*—how they could only have feelings and emotions for the past or the future.

Nathan tried to listen patiently, but it wasn't long before he broke in. "Don't you guys want to do something? Don't you want to fight to get those *now* feelings back?"

"Oh, we had tried in the past," the white-haired man explained. "And we'll try in the future—"

The Out-of-Timers

"But *now*!" Nathan exclaimed. "What about *now*?"

"There was and will be no *now*."

"But . . . don't you see?" Nathan sputtered in frustration. "The future will always become the *now*. And then you won't be able to enjoy it or do anything about it because it's *now*."

The group in the car looked at him blankly.

He tried again. "You will never do or enjoy anything, because when you try to, it will no longer be the future, but it will be the present."

The group shrugged and turned back to their conversation.

"Doesn't anyone care?"

There was no answer.

Josh tried another approach. "Okay, okay, why don't you just tell us where he's going . . . I mean, where he *was* going?"

"Into that swamp," an elderly woman with a fur hat said from the front seat. "When they heard you had arrived, the two of them raced into that swamp."

Joshua and Nathan turned in the direction she pointed. Not far away stretched a huge swamp, so large it could have been a small sea. It was covered with thick vegetation and shrouded in a dark, impenetrable fog.

"In there?" Nathan asked nervously.

"That's right!" the beggar nodded. "They ran in there and someday we will follow."

The other passengers nodded then resumed recalling their past and dreaming of their future.

"Come on," Josh motioned to Nathan, "let's get him."

"In there?" Nathan repeated.

"Of course!"

"By ourselves?"

"I don't see any other volunteers—come on!" Joshua turned and headed for the swamp.

Nathan hesitated a moment, then turned back to the car and tried one last time. "You sure nobody wants to help?"

"Yes, we will help," the white-haired man repeated. "Someday, we will."

Nathan let out a heavy sigh as he realized that "someday" would never arrive . . . and when it did, it would be gone. At last he turned to join his brother, his armor clunking with every step. Strange, the metal suit fit a lot better since their first encounter with the Merchant. Nathan wondered if he'd gained weight or grown a bit. And the shield, it didn't seem nearly as heavy.

But that did little to relieve his fears. The swamp loomed before him just as dark and foreboding as ever. . . .

▣

Back at Master Control one alarm sounded after another.

"What's she doing now!" the Weaver cried in frustration. "Project her image!"

An assistant transferred another image to the center screen. In it Denise, Mr. Hornsberry, and Samson were racing toward a beach.

Behind them was an angry mob, screaming: "GET THE TABLET . . . GET THE TABLET . . . GET THE TABLET . . ."

"Close in on Denise!" the Weaver ordered. "Let's hear what she's saying!"

The assistant obeyed as Aristophenix and Listro Q leaned forward for a better listen. . . .

"Hurry!" Denise shouted as they arrived at the bright, sunny beach and started trudging through the sand. "The beach people will protect us. Look how happy they are!"

The Out-of-Timers

Unlike the wretched souls pursuing them, the crowd on the beach seemed to be having a great time.

"See," Denise cried to Mr. Hornsberry, "not everybody hates what I've done."

The group in Master Control also saw. Actually they saw too much . . . Hundreds of people were staggering about on the beach, screaming, shrieking, drinking, dancing, beating up each other, and . . . well if you could name it, they were probably doing it . . . and worse! It was like a giant out-of-control party.

Mr. Hornsberry shouted over the din, "I fail to fully comprehend what has transpired."

Samson chattered in agreement.

"I added the one thing I'd forgotten!" Denise shouted. "Freedom!" She dodged a couple beer bottles flying in their direction. "If you really want people to be happy, then let them be free to do whatever they want!"

"I understand that you have removed the rules, Miss Denise, but—"

"But it shouldn't be like this!" Denise agreed. "Something's wrong. Something's not—Look out!" She pushed Hornsberry to the side just as a school bus roared past them. It missed the group by mere feet as it slid past, throwing sand over them. The driver of the bus obviously felt he didn't have to obey the road rules. But the screaming, hysterical children inside the bus obviously thought he should.

"What was that about?" Mr. Hornsberry shouted as he staggered to his feet, coughing and brushing himself off.

Before Denise could answer, she spotted a mom and dad pleading with their little five-year-old. Actually, she wasn't so little. In fact, she was as wide as she was tall, and for good reason. She was cramming her mouth with so many chocolate bars that she could barely breathe. The goop covered her face, her hands, her entire body. And still she continued to eat, practically choking as she shoved in one bar after another.

"What are you doing?" Denise demanded. She turned to the parents. "Make her stop! She's going to get sick, make her stop!"

"We're trying!" the father cried. "But since there are no rules, she won't listen to us! She won't stop!"

"GET THE TABLET . . . GET THE TABLET . . ."

Denise threw a look over her shoulder. The angry mob, the hundreds of broken and twisted people, were gaining on them. Before she could respond, another group approached her from the volleyball courts. They were young people. Very *angry* young people.

"We want to talk to you!" Their leader, a blonde-headed surfer, shouted. "We want to talk to you *now*!"

"What's wrong?" Denise asked.

"It's the radio stations," he complained. "They've gone off the air. Nobody wants to work in them anymore!"

"What?" Denise asked.

"And not just the radio stations," a freckle-faced girl in a scant bathing suit complained. "The malls are closed, too. And the theaters!"

"That's right," a boy with bow tie and glasses shouted. "And the hospitals, and the doctors' offices, and—"

"Wait a minute," Denise interrupted. "I don't understand."

"Without rules," the surfer shouted, " nobody wants to do anything, so nobody does anything!"

"But . . . ," Denise stammered. "They have to work . . . they have to eat."

The Out-of-Timers

"Not when they can steal," the girl yelled.

"Steal?"

"Of course! Everybody takes whatever they want from who-ever they want!"

"But . . ." Frustration filled Denise and tightened her throat. "It's not supposed to be like this! Having no rules is supposed to—"

She was interrupted by the roar of the bus. It had spun around and was heading straight for them. The driver behind the wheel was laughing hysterically!

"LOOK OUT!" the young people screamed.

Denise dove to the ground as the bus roared by—missing her by inches. But the teens weren't so lucky. It slammed into the group, running over many of them.

"NO!" Denise shouted.

But thanks to the Tablet, they weren't dead and they felt no pain—though their bodies were smashed and destroyed beyond recognition.

The bus continued to slide until it plowed into a nearby refreshment stand, destroying it and wiping out another dozen people. As it skidded back onto the road it veered too sharply to the left. Tires screeched and smoked, before it finally toppled over, rolling once, twice—the children inside screaming—before it finally settled to a stop onto its back.

The air was filled with dust and the screams of children. They were trapped inside with no way out. Suddenly the engine exploded and caught fire, spewing thick black smoke into the bus. The children coughed and choked. Some tried to crawl out the windows but couldn't. Others pressed their faces to the glass, banging on it, begging for someone to come rescue them.

But no one did.

Denise stared in horror as the smoke filled the bus. She turned to the crowd and cried, "Isn't anybody going to help?"

A nearby lifeguard turned over on his blanket for a better look, but he did not move. A policeman quit his volleyball game and watched with interest. Others drew closer but only for a better view.

Denise was beside herself. "We've got to help them!"

"And ruin the show?" an elderly woman asked as she adjusted her beach chair to see better. "Why should we care?"

"Because they're going to die!"

"People don't die anymore, remember?" the woman said.

"What about their pain?" Denise cried.

"There is no pain," the policeman reminded her.

"You're just going to sit and let the bus burn up?" she screamed.

"Should be fun."

Denise spun back to the bus, hot tears burning her eyes as one child after another began sliding from the windows, overcome with smoke. This wasn't the kingdom she wanted! Nothing was turning out like she'd planned! Nothing at all!

She looked at the Tablet in her hand. If she could just remove some of the commands! But every one was written in the same permanent marking pen. Each and every command was impossible to erase.

Chapter Nine

The Invitation

"Josh . . . Josh, where are you?"

"Over here."

"Where?"

"Right over—ouch! That's my foot!"

"Sorry."

"Ow, that's my other one!"

It was dark in the swamp. So dark that the brothers couldn't see a thing, not even each other.

"This is impossible," Nathan complained as he waded through the thick, smelly ooze that clung and tugged at his every step. Then there was the dense undergrowth of branches that continually slapped him in the face. "How are we supposed to find the Merchant if we can't even see where we—"

"Shh . . . listen."

"I don't hear any—"

"Shhhh."

Nathan did his best to keep quiet. Not an easy trick when you're standing in muck and sinking to your waist, or when it's so dark you can't see, or when you happen to be a world-class whiner. But with great effort he somehow managed to hold off complaining, until he finally heard . . .

"What is that?" he whispered.

"It sounds like . . . panting," Josh whispered back. "Like a giant dog,"

In perfect unison, both boys whispered, "TeeBolt!"

"That means we're right next to them," Josh said.

"But where?"

In the darkness Nathan heard a faint click that sounded like a switch being flipped. Then he heard the gentle sound of falling mist. Suddenly his brother started to whimper:

"How come Imager gave *you* that suit of armor?"

"What . . ."

"It's not fair, you *always* get the good stuff."

"What are you talking about?" Nathan whispered.

"It's just like at home. Mom and Dad always treat you better—"

"Josh—"

"—just 'cause you're the baby."

"What's wrong with you?" Nathan asked. "Joshua?" He heard a faint chuckle just a few feet away and his blood went cold. There was no mistaking its owner.

"Sounds like the Joshua is feeling a little *jealous*," the Merchant's voice taunted. This was followed by more sounds of panting and slurping—obviously from TeeBolt.

"You always get what you want," Joshua complained.

"Where are you?" Nathan whispered to him.

"Just 'cause of that stupid hip of yours—"

"It's the Merchant," Nathan explained, "he's controlling your emotions. Where did he spray you?"

"—everyone's always feeling sorry for you."

Reaching toward Josh's voice, Nathan tried to take hold of him. But he only caught part of his shirt and the water skin hanging around his neck.

"Get back!" his brother shouted as he yanked away.

The shirt slipped through Nathan's armored fingers. So did the water skin. But not before his sharp metal glove ripped a gash into the top of it.

"Now look what you've—"

The Invitation

But that was as far as Josh got before the glow stopped him. The glow of the water. In the utter blackness, the liquid spilling from the tear gave off a faint light.

"It's Imager's words!" the Merchant's voice cried.

Nathan spun around to see the creature just a few feet from them. He was covering his eyes and screaming, "Put it away! Put it away!" He turned and waded deeper into the swamp. "TeeBolt, come!" The giant animal splashed after him. "Not so close, you nincompoop! Not so close!"

Nathan turned back to Joshua. In the faint glow he could see the Merchant's moisture glistening on his brother's arm. "Here," he said reaching toward it, "let me touch that and—"

"Look how you ripped my water skin!" Josh whimpered. "It's no fair. Your stuff always lasts longer than—"

Nathan's glove finally touched the moisture. There was a loud hiss as the emotion boiled off of Joshua's skin. His brother blinked and shook his head as his senses returned.

"Are you okay?" Nathan asked.

"Yeah," he said, giving his head another shake. "Where's—"

There was a distant snapping of twigs. They both turned to see TeeBolt disappear into the darkness after his master.

"Let's get them!" Josh shouted.

"But—"

"We have to stop them before they leave for Earth!"

"But how?" Nathan argued. "We can't see a thing!"

"We've got this water!" Josh held up the water skin with the light glowing from its ripped top. "Come on!"

"But his emotions! They nearly had you again!"

"Just keep fighting them off with that armor of yours," Josh said. "You're doing great!"

"Yeah, but—"

"You defend us with your armor. I'll use this water to light our way. Come on!"

Before Nathan could argue, Josh started into the darkness. He held the water skin out in front of him, preventing any more from spilling out of its torn opening, while using its glow to guide each of their steps.

Their going was much faster now and soon they spotted the Merchant. As usual, he was berating TeeBolt as they stumbled and staggered through the darkness. "No!" the Merchant whispered harshly. "*You're* the pet. *I'm* the master. You go first!"

TeeBolt whined, panted, and slobbered in protest.

"Merchant!" Joshua shouted.

The Merchant spun around and for the first time since they met, Nathan saw fear on the creature's face. "Get away!" he shouted, shielding his eyes against the light of the water skin. "Keep that water away from me!"

"Oh, so this makes you a little nervous, does it?" Josh asked, holding the water out farther.

"Josh," Nathan warned, "be careful."

"That's right," the Merchant threatened as he reached to the Emotion Generator strapped to his chest. "Come any closer and I'll fire."

"We're not afraid of you," Joshua said as he continued to slosh forward in the swamp.

"Have it your way," the Merchant sneered as he flipped another switch.

"Look out!" Nathan cried. Without thinking he leaped in front of Josh to block the mist with his shield. It struck the metal with a violent hiss, then was gone.

The Invitation

"Thanks," Josh grinned. "You're getting pretty good at that."

Nathan grinned back, as amazed as he was nervous.

"Keep your distance," the Merchant warned. "Stay away with that water!" He reached for another switch.

Nathan raised his shield in preparation. Things were starting to make sense now. It was just as the Weaver had said. They each had their weapons. Nathan, his armor—Joshua, his water. And, if they worked together, maybe, just maybe, they could defeat the Merchant.

The creature fired another emotion.

Nathan easily deflected it with his shield.

"Let's get him," Joshua said.

Nathan nodded and they started forward.

"I'm warning you!" the Merchant cried, backing up. He began firing one emotion after another, in rapid succession. But with Josh's light Nathan could see each cloud of mist coming and was able to block it with his shield. As they hit the metal, each evaporated with a sinister hiss.

"TeeBolt!" the Merchant cried. "Attack!"

But TeeBolt was too busy running in the opposite direction to be doing much attacking.

"TeeBolt!"

As the brothers continued toward him Josh held out the water. "Sure you don't want a little drink?"

The Merchant began to tremble. "The Joshua must keep that away. The Joshua does not know its power!"

Nathan was not surprised at the Merchant's fear. He remembered all too well how the water had destroyed his evil sister's Kingdom of Seerlo.

Josh adjusted the rip at the top of the water skin so even more of the glow poured out—the glow that seemed to blind the

Merchant, paralyzing him with fear. "Please"—he covered his eyes—"have mercy, have mercy!"

They were only two steps away now.

The creature dropped to his knees, cowering in fear. "Have mercy, have mercy!"

Josh came to a stop and raised the water skin over the creature's head.

"Please . . . I'll do anything the Joshua asks—please, please . . ."

"Anything?"

"Yes, yes . . ."

"You'll return to your own world? You'll leave the Upside-Down Kingdom alone?"

"Put it away, please—"

Josh repeated, *"You'll leave the Upside-Down Kingdom alone?"*

❑

The children on the bus had all slipped from the windows. And still none of the beach people moved to help. In fact, they actually started to complain.

"That's it? No more explosions? No one is going to catch fire?"

Denise turned to them in astonishment. "Are you crazy? Do you *want* to see awful things?"

"Why not?" the old woman shrugged. "With no work, we need something to do."

"That's right," the lifeguard yelled. "We need some type of entertainment!"

"Yeah," the policeman agreed. "Entertain us. You've taken everything else away, the least you can do is entertain us."

Those around him started to agree. "Yes, entertain us." Others joined in. "Entertain us . . ." They began approaching her. "Entertain us . . . Entertain us . . ."

The Invitation

Denise started to back away.

They grew louder, more demanding, "Entertain us! Entertain us!"

Another set of voices came from behind her:

"GET THE TABLET . . . GET THE TABLET . . ."

Denise whirled around to see the first group from the mansion. They had finally arrived and were also closing in. "GET THE TABLET . . . GET THE TABLET . . ."

"ENTERTAIN US . . . ENTERTAIN US . . ."

Others approached from other directions . . . The father with his chocolate-covered daughter. Pain filled his eyes as he cried out to Denise. "You've made our lives a nightmare . . . a living nightmare!"

Then there were the mangled teens who had been hit by the bus. Some walked, others staggered, many could only drag themselves toward her. "Monsters . . . you've made us monsters . . ."

Tears filled Denise's eyes. "No, I . . . I created good! This is supposed to be good!"

"A NIGHTMARE . . . YOU'VE CREATED A NIGHTMARE . . ."

"ENTERTAIN US . . ."

"MONSTERS, WE'RE MONSTERS . . ."

"GET THE TABLET . . ."

Denise turned, trying to run, but they were coming at her from every side. Angry people, broken people, ruined people.

"ENTERTAIN US . . ."

"NIGHTMARE . . ."

"MONSTERS . . ."

"GET THE TABLET . . ."

"Mr. Hornsberry!" She turned to her friends "Samson—do something! Help me!"

But there was nothing they could do.

The mob closed in. "Don't you understand?" she cried. "I was trying to make things better!" Tears streamed down her face.

"NIGHTMARE . . ."

"MONSTERS . . ."

"YOU MUST BE STOPPED!"

They were nearly on top of her.

She pulled the Tablet closer. "NO! DON'T YOU SEE . . . I JUST, I JUST WANT EVERYBODY TO—" Suddenly, she had an idea. She reached for her marker and began to write.

"STOP HER!" the father screamed.

"GET THE TABLET!"

They lunged for her, but not before Denise had finished writing. She shouted, "I JUST WANT EVERYBODY TO . . ." she spun around the Tablet to reveal the words: *FEEL GOOD*!

⊡

The Merchant of Emotions let out a screeching laugh. "Too late!" he screamed into the boys' faces. "You're too late!"

Instantly, he vanished. Without a trace—except for the giant eight-legged pet who started whining at being left behind.

⊡

Back in Master Control, alarms and lights flashed everywhere.

"What's happening?" Aristophenix cried.

"Wrong, what's?" Listro Q yelled.

"Denise has given the invitation!" the Weaver shouted back.

"What?"

"She's invited the Merchant of Emotions to the Upside-Down Kingdom!"

Chapter Ten

Round One

A shadow fell across the angry mob. They looked up from Denise and into the sky as a huge leather-winged creature blocked the sun, then dove directly toward them.

"It's heading for us!" someone cried.

Others in the crowd screamed as they started running, hobbling, and dragging themselves away.

Denise could only stand, staring. She watched as the creature swooped down in front of her and landed directly behind the people.

"Please," the creature called to them. "I mean the Upside Downers no harm. It is urgent that I speak to the Upside Downers. You must listen to me. . . ."

The pleas sounded earnest and many in the crowd began to slow—

"It is so very important. . . ."

Soon they came to a stop.

"Please . . ."

Some began to turn, listening cautiously to what the creature had to say.

It folded its wings and preened a few crystal scales. The braver and more curious took a step closer. Others followed. When it appeared to have everyone's attention it spoke again.

"I am here to help." The creature tried to look friendly and smile—not an easy job when you have a beak for a mouth.

The group murmured, uncertain, until finally the father of the chocolate-bar eater stepped forward. "Who are you?" he demanded. He was obviously trying to sound courageous. He might have pulled it off if his voice wasn't two octaves higher and shaking like a leaf.

Denise found her own voice. "Don't listen to her!" she shouted. "It's the Illusionist!"

Mr. Hornsberry cleared his throat. "Actually, it's the Merchant of Emo—"

Denise ignored him and stepped closer to the creature. "You're supposed to be dead! We destroyed you in the Sea of Justice!"

The creature turned from the crowd to face her. "The Denise did not destroy me. The Denise destroyed my awful sister—the Illusionist."

"She was your sister?" Denise asked suspiciously.

The creature bowed his head as if embarrassed. "Alas and alack, the Illusionist was the black sheep of the family. And, though her loss caused us great pain, we knew it was for the best." He took a deep breath, his beak trembling slightly. "And for that"—he swallowed—"for that we thank the Denise."

Samson chattered what sounded like a warning, but Denise didn't need anyone to tell her to be careful. "Why are you here?" she asked, taking another step forward. "What do you want?"

"I am the Denise's servant. The Denise summoned me here. What does the *Denise* want?"

"Me?"

"The great Denise summoned me with her wondrous Tablet."

Denise frowned, glancing down at the flat stone in her hand.

Once again the father of the chocolate-bar eater spoke. "Look, Mr., uh . . ."

"Merchant," the creature answered as he turned back to the crowd. "Just call me Merchant."

"Well, Mr. Merchant," the father took a step closer. Others followed behind him. "The point is, Denise here has made our lives unbearable and—"

"Unlivable!" another shouted.

"Impossible!" another cried.

The father continued. "And we've decided we must stop her."

"That's right!" other members of the group agreed. "She must be stopped." They moved closer. "She must be stopped at once!" As they approached, the Merchant reached down and adjusted something strapped to his chest.

"It's the Emotion Generator!" Mr. Hornsberry cried.

"What are you doing?" Denise shouted.

He turned to her and grinned. "Just setting my little machine here to maximum strength."

"Machine?" she asked.

"It's the Emotion Generator, the Emotion Generator!" Mr. Hornsberry cried as he hopped from side to side.

Pointing a nozzle at the angry crowd, the Merchant chortled, "I think it's time they loosen up a bit, don't you?" He flipped a switch and a mist shot out over half of the group. Suddenly they broke into laughter—uncontrollable, backslapping, hold-your-sides laughter. Many dropped to their knees, trying to catch their breath, but it did little good. They couldn't seem to stop.

"What did you do?" Denise demanded. "What was that?"

"Just a little *laughter*," the Merchant chuckled. He redirected the nozzle toward the other half of the crowd. "And how about some *peace* for you folks." He flipped another switch and another cloud of mist shot out, raining down upon the rest of the group. Suddenly, they broke into dreamy smiles. Many closed their eyes, rocking back and forth as if they were in their own world . . . as if everything was perfect with no need to worry about anything.

"Stop him!" Mr. Hornsberry shouted. "He must be—"

The creature spun around and gave both Mr. Hornsberry and Samson a squirt as well.

"Sammy!" Denise shouted. "Mr. Hornsberry!"

But they no longer seemed to hear. If they did, they no longer cared. They simply closed their eyes and broke into mindless smiles.

"What have you done?" Denise shouted at the Merchant. "What have you done?"

"Your humble servant has done nothing," the Merchant replied. "The Denise is the one who invited me. The Denise is the one who commanded that all Upside Downers must feel good."

Denise looked down at the Tablet. It was true, the words *FEEL GOOD* were there just as bold as ever. She looked back to the crowd of laughers. By now they were rolling on the ground, gasping for air. While those hit by the *peace* mist were also sinking to the ground, apparently finding no need to stand.

"How . . . how long will this last?" she asked.

"The Denise wants Upside Downers to feel good, doesn't she?"

"Yes, but how—"

"If that's what the Denise wants, that's what she will get."

"But when will it wear off?"

"I'm afraid, like your Tablet, the effects of my emotions are permanent."

Permanent! The word hit Denise hard. "But . . . they can't get up. They can't go anywhere. They can't do anything!"

"That is correct, the Upside Downers will never go anywhere or do anything again."

"But . . . but they have to eat. They have to—"

The Merchant shook his head. "If the Upside Downers always feel good, why should they?"

Round One

"You mean they'll just—"

"Stay here forever." The Merchant nodded.

"But they'll starve to death."

"The Denise has destroyed death, remember?"

"So they'll just stay here until they . . . shrivel up for lack of food?"

"Or water," the Merchant agreed. "They'll stay here until they turn to dust and simply blow away."

"But . . . you just can't—"

"I have no choice," the Merchant sighed. "The Denise wrote it on the Tablet."

She turned and stepped toward the crowd. "You guys can't sit here like that!" she yelled. "You've got to get up and do something! Get up! Get up!"

Those who bothered to respond only laughed . . . or smiled dreamily.

"Mr. Hornsberry!" She turned to the dog, then to Samson. "Do something!"

But they sat on the sand, smiling away.

Fighting back her panic, Denise turned and walked into the sitting crowd. "What about you?" she shouted at the father who had tried to be the hero. "What about your daughter! Don't you want to save her?"

The man closed his eyes and smiled.

She waded further into the group, toward the laughers. She spotted the teen surfer. "You can't sit here forever!" she shouted. "Don't you want to do something—be something?"

The boy laughed all the harder.

The Merchant sighed. "I'm afraid the Denise has made quite a mess with that Tablet."

She looked around. He was right. What *had* she done? She was supposed to make things better. She was supposed to help their lives, not ruin them. But now . . . now the people were not only twisted and crippled, now they were smiling mindlessly or laughing insanely. By trying to make a dream world, she had, quite literally, created a nightmare.

Angrily she brushed at the tears springing to her eyes. "What am I supposed to do?" she demanded. "How can I make it better?"

"Perhaps . . ." The Merchant looked down to the ground and shrugged. "No, that would never work."

"What?"

"I don't think . . ."

"Tell me!"

"It's just . . . well, if the Tablet were turned over to someone more experienced . . ."

Denise looked at him.

"After all," he continued, "the Denise was right, she did improve upon Imager's work. Once she took charge, things did become better for a while, but . . ."

"But what?"

"The Denise simply did not have the experience."

"And you do?"

Again, he looked to the ground. "I cannot do it on my own, of course not." He gave another shrug. "But together—the Denise with her great understanding of Upside Downers and I with my vast experience—together we could make this the great world the Denise dreamed of."

"And"—Denise motioned to the crowd—"all this will stop?"

"Not only will it stop, but together, we will make this world *perfect*."

Denise looked back at the Tablet in her hands. "But . . . how will I know?"

Round One

Again the Merchant tried to smile. "I guess the Denise will just have to trust me."

She frowned. How? How could she trust him? Look what he did to these people—turning them into mindless zombies, insane laughers. And yet, and yet . . . he was only following orders . . . *her* orders. It really wasn't *his* fault . . . it was *hers*.

The Merchant stepped closer. "The Denise would not give up power," he smiled. "She would simply share it. I will make no decision without the Denise. I give the Denise my word."

Denise felt herself weakening. It wasn't as if she was giving up control—she'd just have a partner. She turned to him and swallowed. "You promise?" she asked.

"Cross my hearts and hope to die." Again he smiled. "Please, just let me touch it. The Denise may hold it, only allow me to touch it."

"And things will be better?"

"Things will be . . . perfect." Gently, the Merchant reached out his claws. "Please . . . it will be for the good of the people—your people."

Denise looked back at the crowd of howling laughers and mindless smilers—a crowd that would remain that way forever unless . . . unless . . .

"For them . . . ," the Merchant whispered sincerely. "For them."

Finally, she began to nod. Then, slowly, she stretched the Tablet toward the Merchant. And just as his claws touched the stone . . .

BEEP!........BOP!........BLEEP!.......BURP!....

. . . Joshua and Nathan appeared. Oh, and one other traveler . . . an eight-legged dog.

As Denise turned toward them, the Merchant took advantage of the distraction and ripped the Tablet from her hands. But his possession was short-lived. For when the dog saw him, it broke into a grin and raced toward him full speed.

"No!" the Merchant cried. "TeeBolt! *Noo!*"

But love knows no bounds. Before the Merchant could stop him, TeeBolt leaped onto him with his front paws (all four of them) and sent them crashing to the ground—TeeBolt, the Merchant, and the Tablet. As they hit the sand, the stone was jarred from his hands.

"Get it!" Josh yelled. "Don't let him have the Tablet!"

The Merchant wiggled toward it—not an easy task with a three-hundred-pound pooch on your chest. "Get off me, you nincompoop! Get off me!" But the sound of the Merchant's voice gave TeeBolt even more joy, making him pant harder, drool gooeyer, and lick wetter. "No, boy!" The Merchant coughed and gagged. "Easy, fella, easy . . ."

Still, his claws were only inches from the Tablet. If he could just touch them. If he could just reach out and—

Denise spotted what he was doing and lunged for the stone . . . just as the Merchant did!

Chapter Eleven

Greed

Nathan watched as Denise and the Merchant rolled back and forth in the sand fighting for the Tablet.

"Let me—"

"It's mine!"

"The Denise doesn't know—"

The Merchant nearly had it in his claws before she yanked it away.

Pulling the marker from her pocket, she started writing the letters, M-I—

"The Denise must give it to me!" The Merchant wrapped his claws around it, ripping it from her hands—just as she finished the word . . . *MINE*.

Suddenly the Tablet flashed white hot and the Merchant dropped it to the sand screaming, "AUGH!"

Denise quickly scooped it up. But in her hands it appeared as cool as always. And Nathan knew the reason. It was the last word she'd written on it. Now, the Tablet would always be hers. Now, nobody would be able to touch it.

"Way to go, Denny!" he shouted.

"Nice work!" Josh agreed.

"We'll see about *nice*," the Merchant sneered as he rose to his feet and smoothed his ruffled scales. "So the Denise doesn't want to share, does she? Fine. If the Denise wants to be greedy, let her be . . . *greedy*." He reached to his Emotion Generator and flipped another switch.

Nathan shouted: "DENNY, LOOK OUT!"

But he was too late. Before Denise could respond, a mist of emotion shot from the Merchant's Generator and covered her entire body.

Suddenly her eyes grew wide with desire. She pointed to the first thing she saw—a nearby beach umbrella. "Mine!" she cried. As if caught in a mighty wind, the umbrella ripped from the sand and flew across the beach until it clattered onto the ground at Denise's feet.

Nathan looked at his brother in astonishment.

She pointed at the next thing she saw—the lifeguard station. "Mine!" she cried. Immediately it tore from its foundation and was at her side. A little tipsy from the sudden move, but there, nonetheless.

The Merchant started to laugh. "If the Denise wants to control the Tablet, let her. I'll simply control the Denise!"

"Mine!" Denise pointed at a pair of sandals on the feet of one of the laughers. Suddenly they were on her feet.

"You can't control her!" Nathan cried.

"Hasn't the Nathan learned yet?" the Merchant laughed. "Whoever controls the emotions controls the person."

"We'll see about that," Josh said, reaching for his water skin. "You may have her now, but not for long."

"Oh, yes, very long. And I'll soon have the Joshua and the Nathan as well."

"No way," Nathan declared, raising his shield and stepping beside his brother. The armor fit much better now. Nearly perfect. "With this shield and that water you can't touch us."

"The Nathan has a point. I can't." He turned to Denise and spoke. "Look at the Nathan's nice shiny armor. Wouldn't the Denise love to have that?"

Denise smiled and pointed. "Mine!"

Immediately the shield was ripped away and the armor torn off. Now Nathan stood only in his underwear.

Greed

"Denny!" he cried. But she didn't hear over the Merchant's laughter.

Suddenly the brothers were defenseless. They still had the water, but without the shield or armor, there was nothing to protect them from the Merchant.

"Let's see," he mused as he looked over the switches strapped to his chest. "What will it be? *Fear*? No, no, we tried that before. An interesting reaction, but not quite the effect we're looking for."

"Listen—" Joshua tried to reason.

But the Merchant wasn't listening. "Ah, here's an excellent choice. How about a little *hopelessness*?"

"A little what?" Nathan asked.

"*Hopelessness*. It's one of my favorites—and soon to be yours."

"Wait!" Josh shouted.

The Merchant flipped the switch.

"No!" Nathan cried, taking a step backwards.

But the mist shot from the Generator and gently rained down upon both of them.

▣

Listro Q!" Aristophenix shouted over the alarms in Master Control.

The purple creature turned to his partner. No words were spoken. Each knew what had to be done. Listro Q reached into his pocket for his Cross-Dimensionalizer.

"No!" the Weaver interrupted. "It's too dangerous."

"Other choice, what have we?" Listro Q asked.

"There's no way of knowing the outcome," the Weaver warned. "The tapestries are unraveled, yes, they are."

"If don't go we," Listro Q said, "then destroyed will be our friends?"

Aristophenix agreed:

93

**Not only our friends,
But all Upside Downers as well.
We gotta stop the Merchant
from casting his spell.**

"You don't understand," the Weaver insisted. "There is nothing I can do if you fall under his power."

Aristophenix nodded.

**We know the risks,
our chances are few.
But they're Imager's Beloved,
what more can we do?**

The Weaver took a deep breath. It was true. The Upside-Down Kingdom was Imager's favorite. No price was too great to save them. Imager had proven that by his own sacrifice for them, the one symbolized by the Blood Mountains. And if Imager was willing to pay such a price, how could he, the Weaver, prevent Listro Q and Aristophenix from doing any less?

The two quietly waited for his decision.

At last he nodded . . . slowly, sadly.

Listro Q entered the coordinates as Aristophenix fired off one last poem:

**Don't worry 'bout us,
we're pros, don't ya know.
Them coordinates, they're a-entered,
so let's get on with the —**

BEEP!........BOP!........BLEEP!.......BURP!....

Greed

. . . and they were gone.

The Weaver stood alone. He could feel a lump growing in his throat, moisture burning in his eyes. Finally he turned back to the screen. "I'm going to miss those poems," he whispered hoarsely, "yes, I am."

Chapter Twelve

A Test of Faith

By the time Aristophenix and Listro Q arrived in the Upside-Down Kingdom, the situation was hopeless . . . literally. The Merchant had fired the mist over the boys and now they felt completely *hopeless*.

"Oh, hello," Nathan greeted them flatly. "Sorry you had to come all this way just to get destroyed."

"Say what you?" Listro Q asked in surprise.

"He's got us," Joshua explained. "The Merchant's too powerful for us to win."

"Well, TeeBolt, what do we have here?" The Merchant chuckled to his panting pet. "More victims. Let me see . . ." He looked down at his switches. "What would be appropriate emotions for nosy, do-gooder Fayrahnians?"

Aristophenix turned to the boys. There wasn't much time to explain.

> **Those are only emotions,**
> **over you that he's tossed.**
> **Don't let 'em control you,**
> **You can still be your boss.**

"It's no use," Joshua sighed.

"It's hopeless," Nathan agreed. "They've got my armor and shield. There's no way we can defend ourselves now."

The Merchant continued surveying his emotion switches. Apparently he was in no hurry. "Let's see, we have *anger, anxiety, apathy* . . ."

A Test of Faith

Aristophenix tried again:

**Don't go by your feelings,
go by what you know.
Trust Imager's promise
that you'll overthrow this here foe.**

"I don't see how," Josh sighed.

"It's hopeless," Nathan repeated.

". . . *bashful, bewildered, bitter* . . ."

Aristophenix turned to Listro Q, hoping he'd have a suggestion, but his partner was as clueless as he. If the brothers refused to believe, how could they force them?

Then there was the little matter of the Merchant and his Generator. ". . . *foolish, frantic, friendly* . . ."

Should they just grab Samson and hightail it back to Fayrah before they, too, got zapped? After all, they didn't create these problems, Denise did. As an Upside Downer it was *her* doing, *her* problem.

And yet, Imager had such love for these people. Come to think of it, so did Aristophenix and his partners. Throughout their journeys together a deep friendship had grown. A friendship so strong that they couldn't just leave the kids—even if it was their fault. No, Aristophenix and Listro Q had to stay. They had to stay and . . . and what?

Suddenly Listro Q's eyes lit up. He stepped toward Joshua. "Water still you have in the water skin?"

"Sure, but look how torn it is," Joshua whined. "Everything's ruined. Nothing's going right. The Merchant got Nathan's shield, he's controlling Denny, you're about to get hit with emotions yourself, everything's just hope—"

"The best defense, is offense," Listro Q interupted as he grabbed the water skin.

". . . *optimistic, outrage* . . . That's it!" The Merchant grinned. "*Outrage* would be nice." He reached to the switch. "Yes, *outrage* would be very nice."

Aristophenix quickly whispered to Listro Q,

> **I don't know what you're planning,**
> **but it better be quick.**
> **'Cause we got 1.8 seconds**
> **'fore he switches that switch.**

Listro Q unfolded the gash at the top of Joshua's water skin.

"Put that away!" the Merchant shouted. "Put that away this instant!"

"What are you doing?" Josh cried. "You're gonna make him madder—he'll make things worse!"

"Listen," Listro Q commanded, "carefully very listen."

"To what?"

But Listro Q didn't answer. Instead, he lifted the water skin over Joshua's head and poured the liquid letters and words over him.

"Stop it!" the Merchant shouted.

Next, he turned and poured some over Nathan's head.

"Stop it!" the Merchant cried. He quickly flipped the switch and fired the *outrage* mist . . . but not before Aristophenix shouted to the brothers:

> **Trust in Imager's words,**
> **what you hear is the truth.**
> **Feelings are fickle,**
> **but his words are absolu—**

A Test of Faith

That was as far as he got before the emotion hit him and Listro Q.

"What are you talking about?" Joshua whined. "What words?"

"Why do I have to explain everything for you!" Aristophenix snapped. "Use your brain for once!"

"Shout don't at them!" Listro Q yelled. He seemed equally as angry.

Aristophenix turned on his friend and shouted back, "Don't tell me what to do you, you . . . pretentious, purple . . . pinhead!"

Listro Q pulled up his sleeves. "Who are you calling purple?"

The Merchant roared with laughter. "So much for Fayrahnian love!" But he didn't laugh long.

"Listen!" Josh cried. "What is that?"

"I don't hear anything," Nathan whined.

"Shhh."

Nathan strained to listen. "It's nothing. Just the wind blowing in the—no, wait a minute. It sounds like . . . is that somebody whispering?"

The Merchant glanced nervously about. "It is nothing. You hear nothing!"

Josh turned to his brother. "Can you make it out?"

Nathan shook his head.

Both boys strained to hear. The words were very quiet. Very small. But they were very, very persistent.

> "You will defeat him."
> "You will defeat him."

"I still can't— "
"Shhh!"

> "You will defeat him."
> "You will defeat him."
> "You will defeat him."

"Can you make it out now?"

"Almost . . ."

<blockquote>
"You will defeat him."

"You will defeat him."
</blockquote>

Nathan's eyes widened. He'd heard that voice once before. Once when Denise was trapped in the Experiment. "Is that . . . ?"

Josh nodded. "Imager. That's what he said when we were at the Center. Those were his *exact* words."

"I hear nothing!" the Merchant scorned.

The voice continued:

<blockquote>
"You will defeat him."

"You will defeat him."

"You will defeat him."
</blockquote>

"It's in the water," Nathan exclaimed. He ran his hand over the liquid letters and words still dripping from his face. "His voice is in this water."

<blockquote>
"You will defeat him."

"You will defeat him."
</blockquote>

"Of course it's in the water," Aristophenix angrily shouted. "It's his words!"

"But it's hopeless," Joshua insisted. "We can't defeat him."

"That's right," Nathan whined. "It's hopeless."

"Exactly," the Merchant sneered. "Trust your feelings. They are truth. Listen to your feelings, not these words."

Nathan turned to the Merchant. As he looked at him and listened, his feelings of *hopelessness* grew stronger. He glanced at

A Test of Faith

Joshua. The expression on his brother's face said he felt the same thing. And as the *hopelessness* grew stronger, the voice of the water grew weaker. . . .

"You will defeat him."
"You will defeat him."
"You will defeat him."

"Why is it fading?" Joshua cried.

It was Listro Q's turn to explode in anger. "Fading not is his voice! Fading is your hearing!"

"What?"

"If trust Imager's words, then will fade the power of feelings! But if trust your feelings, then power will fade of Imager's words!"

"That's right," Aristophenix snapped:

> **The decision is yours**
> **who you'll follow today.**
> **Either Imager's words,**
> **or your feelings obey.**

"Imager's words," Joshua cried. "I want to follow Imager's words, but—"

Suddenly the voice grew louder:

"You will defeat him."
"You will defeat him."

"—but I feel so helpless."

Immediately the voice started to fade.

"No, Josh!" Nathan shouted. "We have to trust his words. His words are what's true."

"You will defeat him."
"You will defeat him."
"You will defeat him."

"But it's . . . it's so hard," Josh complained. "I can't."

Again the words started to fade.

"I know," Nathan cried, fighting against the feeling, "but remember . . . remember how they helped us in the Sea of Justice? How those words saved your life?"

Josh nodded. "Yes."

"And how his power saved me from Bobok's menagerie?"

Josh's voice grew a little stronger. "Yes . . ."

"Stop it!" the Merchant shouted as he fired another shot of *hopelessness* at him.

The mist covered Nathan even more thickly than before. Instantly, he felt himself sliding back into impossible hopelessness. He turned to his brother, pleading helplessly with his eyes for him to take over.

Joshua seemed to understand. He closed his eyes and took a deep breath. He set his jaw and then with great effort spoke. "Remember the way Imager saved Denny from the Experiment?"

"Yes," Nathan groaned, feeling the slightest stir of hope. Then, mustering all of his strength he added, "And how he saved me from the Illusionist."

"Yes," Joshua seemed to grow stronger.

"You will defeat him."
"You will defeat him."

"It's working, Nathan. Don't give up. Let's keep remembering what he's done!"

A Test of Faith

"Fools!" the Merchant shouted. "Your feelings are what is real! Trust your feelings, not some long forgotten—"

"How 'bout his power to reweave Denny?" Joshua exclaimed.

"Or how that water destroyed Keygarp," Nathan said, growing stronger.

"And Seerlo," Joshua added, his strength also increasing.

"You will defeat him."
"You will defeat him."
"You will defeat him."

"Stop it!" The Merchant cried. "Imager is nothing! His promises are noth—"

"No!" Josh shouted, spinning around to face him. "*You* are nothing! *You* will be defeated!"

"You are a fool!" the Merchant moved toward him menacingly. "Prove to me those past memories are real—"

"*Prove?*"

"You're the scientist! Can you touch those memories? Can you prove them?"

"Well . . . no," Josh started to falter. "They're just memories, there's no—"

"We will defeat you!" Nathan interrupted. "Joshua and I will defeat you! Right, Josh?"

Joshua tried to agree, obviously fighting to recover from the last blow.

"Right, Josh?"

His brother turned to him. It was no good. Nathan could see him starting to slip away. But, grabbing his shoulders, Nathan looked him straight in the face. "We can do this!" he shouted. "You and me together . . . Joshua, we can do this!"

He saw a glint of understanding return to his brother's eyes. He nodded to him encouragingly and saw even more strength returning. "Just like Imager told us," Nathan continued. "Together, you and I can do this. Together we can defeat him!"

Slowly Joshua began to nod.

"He's never failed us, has he?" Nathan said. "Not once. Not once!"

Confidence continued returning to Josh. He grew stronger by the second.

"Lies!" the Merchant shouted. "You are liars!"

At last Joshua's strength had returned. He spun back on the Merchant and shouted, "No, you're the liar! Imager's words have *never* failed!"

"You will defeat him."
"You will defeat him."
"You will defeat him."

"They destroyed the Illusionist!" Nathan yelled.

"That's right!"

"They destroyed Bobok!"

"Yes!"

"They destroyed Seerlo!"

Josh took a step toward the Merchant. "And they'll destroy you!"

The words were louder than ever:

"You will defeat him."
"You will defeat him."
"You will defeat him."

A Test of Faith

With full confidence, Joshua took the water skin from Listro Q and unfolded the gash at the top of it.

"What are you doing?" the Merchant demanded.

He began approaching the Merchant.

"Stay back! Stay away!" the Merchant ordered.

Nathan joined his brother's side and together they continued forward.

The Merchant backed away. "I'm warning you. Stay away with that!"

The brothers closed in.

In desperation the Merchant turned to his faithful companion. "TeeBolt—TeeBolt, attack!"

But TeeBolt was doing what he did best—running for his life in the opposite direction.

Now the Merchant was only a few feet away. Joshua held out the water skin. "I think it's time for you to leave our world."

"But I like it here," the Merchant hissed. Before Joshua could stop him, he fired off another volley of *hopelessness*. And another. And another.

Both brothers staggered under the impact.

"There's plenty more where this came from!" the Merchant shouted.

Imager's voice started to fade.

"Josh!" Nathan yelled. "Water . . . we need more water!"

Josh raised the water skin and poured it over his head.

The voice grew louder.

He tossed the skin to Nathan, who followed suit.

In a panic the Merchant twirled to Denise. "The Denise must do something! The Denise must write—"

But apparently Denise already had a plan. Still consumed with *greed*, she pointed to the water in Josh's water skin. "Want!"

Immediately the rest of the water was sucked from the skin and dumped onto her. From head to toe the liquid letters and words washed over her. She coughed and gasped, trying to catch her breath.

And for the first time, she also heard Imager's voice.

"You will defeat him."
"You will defeat him."
~~"You will defeat him."~~

"Listen to his words!" Nathan shouted to her. "Trust his words. Trust his words, not your feelings!"

"DON'T BELIEVE THEM!" the Merchant shrieked. "I CAN GIVE YOU ANYTHING YOU WANT."

Denise turned to him.

"JUST NAME IT. WE'RE PARTNERS, REMEMBER?"

She started to nod.

"NO, DENNY!" Josh cried. "NO!"

The Merchant grinned.

"DENNY! DON'T!" Nathan pleaded. "DON'T TRUST HIM! LISTEN TO THE IMAGER'S WORDS!"

Slowly Denise raised her hand and started to point. The Merchant's grin broadened. "Anything, my dear . . . just name it, anything at all!"

"DENNY—NO!" Nathan raced toward her, but Josh grabbed him, holding him back.

"Let me go, let me—"

"It won't do any good, *she* has to decide! Remember what Aristophenix said."

"But—"

"It has to be *her* decision."

A Test of Faith

Nathan looked at his brother, then reluctantly stopped struggling. Of course, he was right. It was up to Denise. He turned to watch as she opened her mouth. She spoke only three words. "That . . . ," she said, pointing at the Emotion Generator. "I want!"

Immediately the Generator was ripped from the Merchant's chest and resting in her arms.

"GIVE THAT BACK TO ME!" the Merchant cried.

"All right, Denny!" Nathan shouted. "Way to go!"

"GIVE THAT BACK TO ME, NOW!" The Merchant started toward her but hesitated as he saw that she was still dripping with Imager's water. "GIVE IT TO ME!"

"I won't give you this," she said looking down at the Generator and scanning the row of switches. "But I might have something else."

"What are you doing?" The Merchant started backing up. "Put that down! You don't know how to use it!"

Spotting a particular switch, Denise smiled. Then she pointed the Generator's nozzle toward the Merchant.

"The Denise doesn't know what she's doing! The Denise doesn't—"

Finally she fired a jet of mist.

"NOOO . . . !"

It fell gently over the Merchant.

"NO!" he screamed. "NO! NO! NO!" He began running in tight little circles. "NO, I DO NOT FEEL THIS! I DO NOT FEEL THIS!"

The brothers looked on in wonder as the Merchant continued to shriek in agony. Finally he unfurled his leathery wings.

"How 'bout one for the road?" Denise asked as she fired another volley onto him.

"NOOO!" he screamed. He flapped his wings and rose off the ground. "NO! NO! NO!" Then he turned, and with several powerful thrusts, headed off into the sky. "NO, NO, NO!" He grew smaller and smaller until he finally disappeared altogether. Only the faint echo of his cries remained. "No, no, nooooo . . ."

Nathan turned to Denise, and before he knew it, he was racing toward her and throwing his arms around her. "Denny!"

Soon his brother joined them in the hug.

"Come on, guys," she coughed, "knock it off. I can't breathe, I can't breathe."

But they had never bothered to let her have her way before, why should they start now?

"You okay?" Joshua asked as they finally separated. "You feeling okay now?"

"*Feelings?*" she said. "I don't know, I wouldn't put too much trust in *feelings*, would you?"

Josh broke out laughing. "No, I guess not."

Nathan joined in the laughter; so did Denise. It felt good. It had been a long time and it felt very good.

"But what did you zap him with?" Nathan asked. "What type of emotion could cause him so much pain?"

"Oh that's easy," Denise grinned. "I got him with the one he hated most."

"Yeah?" Josh asked. "Which is . . ."

Denise's grin broadened. "I nailed him with . . . *love.*"

Chapter Thirteen

Another Day, Another Saved Planet

It didn't take long for Denise to get things back to normal. After all, she still had the Tablet—she still was the boss.

With a few strokes of her trusty pen, everyone in the group was back to their usual selves. Although they all seemed grateful, Mr. Hornsberry was particularly pleased, since it's tough to be a snob when you're sitting on the ground grinning like an idiot.

Denise sighed as she handed Aristophenix the Generator of Emotions. "Here," she said. "Do whatever you need to get rid of this thing, will you?"

> **I'll dispose of it quickly,**
> **on that you can depend.**
> **As of now the Merchant's power**
> **is officially at an end.**

"I tell you," Nathan said, "if I never feel another emotion, it will be too soon."

Listro Q shook his head in disagreement. "Good are emotions."

"He's right," Aristophenix said:

> **Emotions are swell,**
> **'cause they help us to deal**
> **with life's ups and downs.**
> **So it's good that we feel.**

Listro Q nodded. "Like instruments on dashboard. Emotions us tell inside what is happening to our minds."

Nathan frowned. "You lost me on that."

Joshua gave a shot at translating. "You're saying emotions are like gauges that tell us what's happening inside our minds?"

Listro Q agreed. "Gauges and thermometers of your mind are they."

Josh nodded then added, "We just have to make sure we're using them and they're not using us."

"Correct are you."

"Excuse me . . . excuse me, please?"

Denise turned to see the father of the chocolate-bar eater. Behind him stood the hundreds of people who had been on the ground laughing and smiling. Their uncontrollable emotions were now under control, but many of their bodies were still impossibly ruined.

"There's a lot more that has to be done," he said, motioning to the crowd. "We still need your help."

Denise nodded as she looked over the crowd. He was right, things were still a mess. A huge mess. She took a deep breath, sighed, and muttered half to herself, "Where to begin . . ."

"All things make, as used to be they," Listro Q said.

"You mean like Imager had it before I fixed up things?"

"Sounds like a pretty good deal to me," Josh said.

A murmur of approval swept through the crowd.

"But how?" Denise asked. "I mean, if I give them back pain, they'll all suffer. If I give them death, lots of them will immediately die. And what about all those rules I took away?" She sighed again and looked down at the Tablet. "I tell you, it would be better if I'd never even found this thing."

"Precisely," Listro Q agreed.

She looked at him. "What?"

Another Day, Another Saved Planet

"That very thing can happen make you."

"You're not serious?"

Aristophenix nodded:

> **None of this would be,**
> **if the Tablet never was.**
> **So write, 'It never existed,'**
> **and see what it does.**

"But . . . ," Denise protested, "then I won't have the power to make things happen."

"Correct are you," Listro Q said. "Then rely on Imager only must you."

"But . . ."

"Live by his plan, your only option."

"But—"

Aristophenix added:

> **Either you trust him or don't,**
> **the decision is plain.**
> **Either Imager's the boss,**
> **or this insane life remains.**

Denise turned back to the crowd. Things *were* insane, he was right about that. She'd only made a few changes, written a few little words, and look what had happened. She had tried to help these people, but had nearly destroyed them. Instead of perfect people, she had turned them into out-of-control monsters. Monsters who now stood silently waiting, hoping she'd make the right decision.

Denise hated the thought of losing control. But worse, she hated the thought of keeping it. It's true, there were thousands of things she didn't understand about Imager's ways. She probably never would. But she did know one thing—at least she did now. His ways were a *whole* lot better than hers.

Finally she brought the felt pen up to the board. "Well," she said with another sigh, "it's been real."

"Too real," Josh grinned back.

The others chuckled nervously as they waited.

"I guess I'll see you around," she said to the Tablet.

"Or not," Nathan corrected.

She nodded, "Or not." Then quickly and deliberately she wrote the words: THE TABLET DOESN'T EXIST.

◙

Denise woke with a start. For a minute she didn't know where she was—until she felt the jab of a steel armrest in her ribs, the sticky vinyl against her arms, and the cramp in her neck.

Ah, yes, the hospital chair.

She looked over at her mother, who was still asleep—the sedative was still working. In fact, in the dim morning light she actually looked kind of peaceful.

But something had changed. Denise felt it immediately. Her anger about Mom was gone. She wasn't sure why. Maybe it had something to do with that strange dream she'd just had. Talk about weird.

She heard a gentle clearing of throats and looked up to see Joshua and Nathan standing in the doorway.

"Guys?" she said as she rose, struggling to stand.

"Sorry we couldn't come last night," Josh whispered as they stepped inside. "We had to watch Grandpa's store."

"How's she doing?" Nathan asked as he limped past Denise to look at her mother.

"Pretty good."

Another Day, Another Saved Planet

"You stay here all night?" Josh asked.

"Yeah," Denise said, rubbing her stiff neck. "It wasn't too bad. Except for the dream . . . talk about weird."

The boys exchanged glances.

"The *dream*?" Josh asked.

"Yeah . . . it was all about this flat stone, and me writing on it, and—"

"Was there a creature in it?" Josh asked. "Some guy with a machine strapped to his chest?"

"Well . . . yeah. How did—"

"And an eight-legged dog?" Nathan asked.

"How'd you guys know?"

Again the brothers traded looks.

Josh cleared his throat. "Nathan had the same dream."

"*What?*"

"So did I."

"You're kidding!" Denise exclaimed.

Her mother stirred slightly.

Nathan lowered his voice, "We both had it last night."

"You mean we all three dreamed the same dream?"

"About a Tablet," Josh said.

Denise nodded. "And some creep trying to take over the world."

"And you ruling it instead of Imager."

Denise leaned against the wall to steady herself. On the weird-ness scale this was . . . well, it was off the scale. *Way* off. "How?" she finally asked. "Why?"

No one had an answer.

Then she asked another question, one she figured they were all thinking. "This has something to do with the Fayrahnians, doesn't it?"

"Probably," Josh answered.

Nathan agreed. "Next time we see them, we'll have to ask."

"Yeah." Denise nodded. "We'll have to." But even as she spoke and glanced back at her mother, she suspected that she knew. Somehow deep inside, she already knew.

◙

Meanwhile, somewhere between the Upside-Down Kingdom and Fayrah, roly-poly Aristophenix, purple Listro Q, and the feisty Samson were cross-dimensionalizing home.

So bits and pieces, only they'll remember? Listro Q thought to Aristophenix.

Aristophenix nodded:

> **A foggy dream**
> **is all they'll recall.**
> **But it'll help in their growth,**
> **of giving Imager all.**

Aristophenix folded his arms in satisfaction. As the leader of the group, he was pleased with the way he'd pulled things off.

Actually, he was very pleased.

Only one question to ask have I, Listro Q thought.

Ask away, my good man, Aristophenix thought back. *Ask away.*

If normal, is back to everything . . .

Yes . . .

Then—Listro Q pointed past Aristophenix—*why a new companion have we?*

What new companion? Aristophenix thought as he turned. *We don't have a new—*

Suddenly he was hit by a galloping eight-legged dog. Before

Another Day, Another Saved Planet

he could be stopped, the grateful animal hopped on Aristophenix's chest and began slurping, licking, and drooling.

Easy, fella! Aristophenix coughed. *Down, boy . . .*

Samson and Listro Q started to laugh.

Come on, fella . . . easy now . . . somebody call him off, call him off!

Although his buddies struggled to pull the animal away, there was something about their continual laughter that told Aristophenix they weren't trying all that hard. Yes, sir, by the looks of things, it appeared TeeBolt had found himself a brand-new master. And, by the looks of things, it appeared he would remain glued to Aristopohenix's side (drool and all)—traveling with him wherever he went . . . even on their future visits to three very special friends in the Upside-Down Kingdom.

Come on, fella . . . get down . . . easy now . . . easy . . .

About the Author

Bill Myers is the author of the humorously imaginative *The Incredible Worlds of Wally McDoogle* series. Bill's latest works include the creation of a brand new secret agent series for early readers, *Secret Agent Dingledorf*. He is also the creator and writer of the *McGee & Me!* video series. Bill is a director as well as a writer, and his films have won over forty national and international awards. He has written more than 50 books for kids, teens, and adults. Bill lives with his wife and two daughters in Southern California.

You'll want to read them all!

The Imager Chronicles

*Who knew that the old rock found forgotten in an attic
was actually the key to a fantastic alternate world?*

When Denise, Nathan, and Joshua stumble into the land of
Fayrah, ruled by the Imager—the One who makes us in His
image—they are drawn into wonderful adventures that teach them
about life, faith, and the all-encompassing heart of God.

BOOK ONE

THE PORTAL

Denise and Nathan meet a myriad of interesting characters in the wondrous world they've discovered, but soon Nathan's selfish nature—coupled with some tricky moves by the evil Illusionist—gets him imprisoned. Denise and her new friends try desperately to free Nathan from the villain, but one of them must make an enormous sacrifice—or they will all be held captive!

BOOK TWO

THE EXPERIMENT

When amateur scientist Josh unexpectedly finds himself whisked away to Fayrah with Denise, he quickly sees that not everything can be explained rationally as he watches Denise struggle to grasp the enormity of the Imager's love. It's not until they meet the Weaver—who weaves the threads of God's plan into each life—that they both discover that understanding takes an element of faith.

BOOK THREE

THE WHIRLWIND

Once again the mysterious stone transports the three friends to Fayrah, where they find themselves caught between good and evil. When Josh falls under the spell of the trickster Illusionist and his henchman Bobok—who convince him that he can become perfect—Denise and Nathan must enlist the help of Someone who is truly perfect before they lose Josh in the Sea of Justice. Will help come in time?